Coming Home

♥♥♥Welcome to Seagull Bay♥♥♥

A brand new cosy English seaside town romance series brimming with friendships. These heartwarming stories find familiar characters returning time and time again, where every new blossoming romance sees townsfolk of varying ages finding love.

After receiving a heart-wrenching letter from her aunt, Pippa found herself hastily packing her bags and embarking on a poignant journey back to the coastal town she once called home in her little Mini car with her faithful pet retriever by her side. Little did she know that a surprising twist awaited her. Within minutes of arriving, she stumbled upon Oliver, her childhood sweetheart, leaving her speechless. Due to his parents' divorce and his move to America, years had passed since they last saw each other, making their reunion all the more unexpected. Pippa believed she had moved on from Oliver during their time apart, convinced that their paths would never cross again. But as she locked eyes with the now strapping six-foot-two man before her, her heart raced and her knees weakened. In that moment, she realised the depth of her foolishness in assuming she had conquered her emotions.

To complicate matters further, Pippa found herself working alongside "the one that got away" in her family's business. As they navigated their shared responsibilities, Pippa grappled with an internal struggle. She still had feelings for Oliver, which were messing with the very important family decision she was yet to make.

Should she set aside her reservations with Oliver and prioritise what is right for her family? Or run back to the safety of Ireland?

Dedication

To my wonderful friends 'The Bakers,' Colin and Ruth.
❤Happy 40th wedding anniversary ❤
I couldn't'wish to know a nicer, more generous and loyal couple than you.
Thank you Ruth, for introducing and taking me to Staithes in Yorkshire.
It's a hidden treasure, and exactly how I envisioned Seagull Bay to be when I wrote this book.

*

Also to Paul Watters for letting me use one of his recipes in my story.
Thank you.

*

Author's note

Check out the recipe used in the story at the end, courtesy of renowned chef Paul Watters. There is a version of it to make for your fur babies, too.

*

Copyright

Copyright © 2023 by Michelle Hill
All events, places, businesses and characters in this publication are clearly fictitious and any resemblance to real persons, living or dead will be purely coincidental. They are all a product of the author's imagination.
ISBN: 9798850545819

Seagull Bay residents of book 1

Ginger · Pippa · Oliver · Jess

Brett · Aunt Morgan · Laurel & Hardy · Declan · Pharis

Old Po · Katherine · Ned · Reverend Townsend · Ava

Mina · Hayley · Ben · Tom · Christine

Act 1 - Chapter one

Driving along the coastal road adjacent to Seagull Bay, Pippa felt a wave of nostalgia as she inhaled the fresh salty sea breeze blowing in through the inch-wide gap in her car window. The bay was famous for seagulls in their hundreds nesting on the cliff faces on either side of it, and some of them flew alongside her car squawking excitedly.

She'd left her apartment in Ireland the previous evening to travel through the night and arrive in her hometown early the next morning. Tired, her concentration was wavering as she fought to suppress the emotions that had been building inside over the last few days.

Pippa passed a road sign showing a layby was coming up ahead, and she took the opportunity for a quick pit stop. Tears were brimming on her lower lashes, making it almost impossible to drive another metre safely, let alone the final mile left of her journey. She hadn't been home for almost two years and she had no intention of turning up an emotional wreck.

As soon as her little Mini came to a standstill, Pippa turned off the engine and rooted in her handbag for the pocket-sized pack of tissues she always kept for moments like this. She pulled one from the small plastic sleeve and dabbed away the tears ready to spill onto her cheeks from in the corners of her eyes, whilst sniffing away a sob.

She turned her head and looked across at Ginger her beloved golden retriever, sitting in the passenger seat, named after the wonderful gingerbread her mother used to bake and sell in their family-owned pub and hotel, right up until her passing just three years ago.

The name seemed inappropriate when Ginger was a puppy, as his fur was snowy-white, but as he'd gotten older, it had turned into a rich golden tan colour. Now it was perfect.

Ginger tilted his head sideways, studying Pippa with dark brown dewy eyes and made a small whimpering noise, as if sympathising with his sad mistress. Pippa reached across and rubbed the soft, short fur on her pet's warm ears and the tightness in her chest eased slightly.

'I'm okay boy...really I am.'

Ginger turned his head and licked the inside of Pippa's wrist.

Pippa drew in a long, jittery breath. Was she? Was she okay? This was the first time she'd been home in such a long time. She loved her childhood home dearly, but ever since her mother's passing, she had found it difficult to go back there. It was haunted by her mother's absence, even though her father had taken to filling every wall with photographs of her beautiful mother.

Yet, instead of the photographs making Pippa celebrate the love she had for her mother, they were a constant reminder to her of how much she missed her.

Pippa kept just one photo of her mother on display in her Irish apartment, yet three years on from losing her beloved mother, her eyes still avoided it at all costs. She still found it much too painful to be reminded of her loss.

Pippa had moved to Ireland two years ago, and it had been one of the hardest decisions of her life. She hated the fact that she'd moved so far away from her father, but she was comforted by the fact she hadn't totally abandoned him. Her Aunt Morgan who had worked with her parents her entire life was there. Her father ran the family and pet orientated pub while Aunt Morgan oversaw the accounts and helped with the hotel side of the business.

Her aunt had always lived close to the pub, and in the last weeks of her mother's illness, her aunt had dutifully moved into the spare bedroom to help care for her. She just never left.

The pub had been their home for as long as Pippa could remember. Her bedroom had always been at the back, with dual aspect windows, while her brother preferred the bedroom next to the family bathroom. The spare bedroom was slightly smaller than the other bedrooms, but it was the warmest and cosiest being next to where the boiler tank was kept. With a sloping ceiling that had a skylight window, it was the perfect room to see the stars whilst lying in bed at night.

After her mother's passing, Aunt Morgan had insisted in staying on and offering her help with early morning deliveries and whatnot on behalf of her grieving brother-in-law. Pippa had taken comfort and felt far less guilty about her move to Ireland, knowing the rock of the family was there 24/7 to aid her father. With her weekly video calls back home, her aunt was never too far away. She got to catch up with both of them at the same time.

Returning to her childhood home and knowing her mother wouldn't be there was an emotional battle. That was why her visits home were few and far between. It was the letter that had drawn her his time.

Pippa reached into her bag, withdrew an envelope, and sat motionless whilst she stared at the familiar cursive writing.

The letter had dropped onto her doormat just days ago, and it had been the catalyst for her emotional upheaval and recent periodic tears from the moment she'd read the second paragraph.

Since receiving it, Pippa had been walking around a ghost of herself. Its contents still shocked her, but after the shattering news had sunk in, she'd immediately booked a ferry ticket back to the small coastal town she'd grown up in. Now she was back in England and just a mile from Seagull Bay.

She needed to pull herself together. Her father needed her. That was the sole reason for coming back home. She pulled the letter out from inside the envelope, unfolded it, and read it again for the umpteenth time.

My dearest Pippa,

I've tried to get hold of you on the phone, but you are as elusive as always and you know how I feel about leaving one of those darn voice mails or texts, so I've gone old school and put pen to paper. I can picture you wrinkling up your nose just like you used to do as a little girl at receiving a letter instead of an email or text, but quite frankly, I think personal matters of such magnitude should be delivered in a more intimate way. Hence the letter.

I'm sorry to be the bearer of bad news, but your father was diagnosed with the early stages of vascular dementia just after you left for Ireland. I don't want you to go into panic mode because he was immediately prescribed tablets that are slowing down the disease, but I need to make you aware his condition is still slowly deteriorating.

He didn't, and still doesn't want you to know about the diagnoses. You know how stubborn he can be, but please don't fret. Like I said, it's progressing slowly, but I have noticed a difference with his forgetfulness these last few weeks.

For now, I've commandeered my friend's son to help out in the pub, which thankfully coincided with one of your father's arthritis flare-ups, so your father will be none the wiser. However, this extra help is only temporary, as my friend's son has his own business to tend to.

I suppose by now you have guessed why I am writing to you, and why I'm dumping this shocking news on you. Your father and I need help running the pub until I can persuade him to retire and sell up, or until I can hire someone else. The part-time cook we have is leaving and as I'm already dealing with the hotel and administration side of the business, I know I'm going to struggle. With the limited use of my legs, I'm already restricted with what I can physically do to help with the hotel and the catering, and I don't want the business to suffer.

I really hate to lumber this on you my dear Pippa, but with your brother serving overseas and with you thankfully being able to work from anywhere as long as you have your laptop and a Wi-Fi connection, your father and I could really use your support. At least until I can persuade the old boy it's time to throw in the towel, retire and sell up. If that fails, just until I can hire someone long-term.

When you come back home, or should I say if you decide to come back—whatever you do, do not let him know I asked you for your help, and don't let on you know about his condition either.

You don't have to answer with a handwritten letter, lol, a text will do. I'm not averse to reading them.

I really hope to see you soon, Kiddo.

All my love, Aunt Morgan.

Pippa folded the letter and slid it back inside the envelope, returning it to the safety of her bag. She inhaled a deep breath and pressed the start button to turn the engine back on as she exhaled loudly.

From her parked viewpoint on the hill, she could just make out the bundle of houses and business in the distance below, surrounded by a patchwork of fields and hills. Some were still green, others had turned brown, and some even had patches of snow, which had been trying to fall again since she left the ferry, even though it was unusual to see snow at this time of year.

A few rogue snowflakes flurried in through the small gap at the top of her window, making Pippa shiver and close it. Fatter flakes fell on the window screen, instantly melting on the warm glass after being continuously blasted by hot air from the car heating. Ginger barked and Pippa laughed, happy to be distracted from her current thoughts.

'I know you love snow Ginger, but I can't let you out here. Just a few more minutes and you'll be able to find a patch to roll around to your heart's content.' Ginger tilted his head, listening intently to Pippa. 'Come on, boy... Let's go home.'

Pippa lifted the indicator stick and edged out of the layby, making sure the road was clear before continuing on to Seagull Bay.

She lowered the window on the passenger side another inch, letting more of the fresh salty sea air infiltrate the car. There just wasn't any other smell like it.

Ginger stuck his wet black nose up against the window, wagging her tail furiously, and Pippa glanced across at her beloved pet and smiled. She pressed the button on the main control panel on her door and the passenger window rolled down a few more inches.

Cold air with the distinguishable aroma of the sea blasted in, and Ginger thrust his nose out through the larger gap, sniffing loudly.

It had been an age since Pippa had been back home. Ginger had been just a pup when she was last there. Now he was fully grown. He barked his excitement. He hadn't forgotten the smell of home…Pippa certainly never would.

The last time she was there, Pippa and Ginger had spent practically every spare minute at the cove in Seagull Bay. It was her favourite place on the beach and just a stone's throw from the family pub.

She had returned home for a wonderful two-week stay in the pub's best hotel room. Her father had questioned why she hadn't wanted to stay in her own bedroom, but she couldn't exactly tell him seeing all the photos of her mum covering every wall and surface of their home was too painful. Instead, she'd opted for a white lie and had told him she wanted Ginger to experience a proper holiday—hotel room included.

Thankfully, her father hadn't caused a fuss; he'd insisted they stay in the best hotel room, which had a specially designed mini four-poster bed for dog guests. Her family's business was, in her opinion, the best dog friendly pub-hotel of any Yorkshire coastal town.

A mile later, Pippa turned onto the road heading to Seagull Bay. Her stomach churned. It was a mix of excitement at being home again and trepidation at seeing how much change there might be in her father.

She passed familiar houses, all painted in different colours, and was amazed to see some rooftops had a smattering of snow. The last time she was here, window boxes had been abundant with flowers, but today they were bare. Just a smattering of powdery snow covered the soil inside them.

Ginger's head turned excitedly from left to right as if recognising where they were and his panting soon misted the door window and the windowscreen on his side of the car. Pippa had to fully lower the passenger side window to be able to see the cars parked outside the houses they passed in the tight winding main street which descended into the heart of the coastal town.

A unique smell of home cooking wafted into the car, and Pippa inhaled slowly and deeply, prolonging the yummy experience. Her tummy rumbled, reminding her she hadn't eaten yet today.

The inviting aroma was coming from a small cafe, which her aunt Morgan had enthusiastically told her about. Pippa was yet to sample its wares, as the open day had been just after she'd departed for her new home in Ireland.

Should she dare try it now just metres from her childhood home? Before she'd even said hello to her father? She smiled at Ginger. It was still early. Her father would most probably only just be rising.

The café's had charming gingham blue curtains, but it was the wooden bone-shaped sign hanging in front of the intricate lace-covered window that sold it to her.

DOGS ARE WELCOME

Pippa turned to Ginger with a grin and ruffled his fur. 'Hungry boy?'

COMING HOME TO SEAGULL BAY   17

Ginger woofed.

Driving around the town's small beachfront, Pippa parked her Mini in the only available spot just outside the small post office shop and turned off the engine. She unclipped Ginger's safety harness and attached his lead to his collar ready to climb out. But Ginger was eager. He jumped over the gear stick and bounded out of her door.

'Yes, someone is definitely hungry,' she giggled.

Locking the car, Pippa walked over to the safety handrail and looked down at the six-feet drop onto the beach below and then out to sea. She'd missed that view. She did a 360-degree turn to take in the cliffs on either side of the small town and smiled up at the seagulls circling.

It looked different, but the last time she'd been here it had been summer. Now the beachfront looked like a scene from a perfect spring-day post card.

The façades of the houses on the beachfront were adorned with charming little garden ornaments on their windowsills and some even had crocheted bunting with different themed pictures knitted into them, strung over their front doors. The pictures on the bunting were of colourful flowers and animals. Her mouth hitched when she saw and recognised crocheted pictures of local food and beverages.

Pippa sighed contentedly. Even the handrail going down on the beach had bunting attached to it. She wondered what was with all the quaint and ornate decorating. There hadn't been anything like this on her previous visit. Had there been a best dressed house competition or something recently? Or was this the new beachfront norm to attract more visitors to the small coastal town? She hoped it was the latter. She'd had the perfect childhood growing up here.

After breaking up for the summer holidays from their small community school when she and her brother were children, the long hot summers had been spent making sandcastles on the beach, and exploring the rocks and caves close by. While she'd had picnics on the soft sand with her friends, her brother had opted for beach bar-b-ques. There had been maypole dancing, orienteering, and plenty of rambling days in their teens.

Pippa's smile curled higher remembering those happy memories as she looked around. These added aesthetic adornments would make childhood for any children living there even more magical than hers had been.

She would have been rooted to the spot for a while longer, taking in the charming beauty of the beachfront if it hadn't have been for Ginger tugging her towards the cafe. 'Okay, okay. I'm coming.'

As she opened the door, Ginger enthusiastically pushed his nose in the gap and barged in his shoulders, flinging the door open and tugging Pippa in after him. She was only two steps into the cafe when she banged into someone's hard chest, almost knocking the wind out of her.

Her apology was already leaving her lips before she untangled herself from the person. 'I'm so sorry. It was my do—'

Pippa stared up into dark brown eyes that had a familiarity about them, yet she didn't recognise the handsome face they belonged to because a thick black beard and moustache covered most of it.

'Pippa?'

Pippa frowned and squinted her eyes. 'Sorry, do I know you?'

'It's Oliver...Oliver Oney.'

Pippa felt her cheeks instantly flush with heat.

Oliver.

Why hadn't she recognised him? She was mortified. They had dated in high school, but their relationship had only lasted for nine months and ten days before he'd dumped her. She still had the calendar buried away somewhere in her bedroom marked off with a love heart for everyday they had dated. She'd carried a torch for him for the rest of her time in school. Right up until she'd left six form for university.

But no matter how many boys she'd tried talking to, or the odd date she was made to go on by her university friends, she'd never been able to get over Oliver—no one ever lived up to him.

When she'd finished university a much more confident young woman and returned to Seagull Bay with a newfound determination to get to the bottom of their break-up, and maybe try to re-ignite their old romance, his parents had divorced and he'd gone to live with his father in America.

She'd been devastated. He was the one who got away. She'd dated on and off over the years and even thought a brief relationship with the lovely Dan from the next village over might have burned hotter than it did—maybe even develop into something deeper. Alas, it never did, so her career became her new love.

But Oliver—she'd often thought of him over the years—especially as she *never did* find out why he'd broken up with her.

'Oh, Oliver...I-I can't believe it's you. You-you look so...*mature*.'

Oliver grimaced and then grinned. 'Is that a polite way of saying I look old with this facial hair?'

Pippa shook her head vehemently. She hadn't noticed at first, but he had a slight American drawl. It was quite mysterious and dare she say it—sexy. 'No, not at all... It's been such a long time since I saw you last. How many years has it been?'

'Sixteen,' Oliver quickly offered. Pippa gasped. Oliver shrugged and smirked. 'I-I've got an excellent memory.'

Ginger yanked on the lead. 'Okay boy, I'm coming.'

Oliver pointed down at Ginger. 'Lovely colour. I have a black Labrador.'

Ginger tugged again. 'Thank you. Maybe I'll get to see your dog while I'm back home?'

'Bitch!'

Pippa's eyebrows shot up. 'I beg your pardon?'

'Sorry if that sounded rude. I meant she's a girl dog—a bitch, not a dog. My girl is called Jess.'

'Ohhh, right...erm, that's a lovely name.' Ginger whined and tugged again. 'I'd better go. He'll have my arm out of its socket soon if I keep him from eating.'

Oliver nodded and smiled. She couldn't help but notice how his dazzling smile made her pulse race. 'I hope to see you very soon, Pippa.'

Pippa thought to herself, *thank goodness God decided to put hearts inside bodies, otherwise Oliver would be able to see how much he's affecting mine right now.*

She smiled, nodded and then headed for the counter, feeling very hot all of a sudden, which was strange because she had been shivering outside a moment ago.

Chapter two

A woman wearing an iced cupcake themed apron, with salt and peppered hair and wrinkles in the corners of her smiling eyes came from behind the counter to stoop down and pet Ginger.

'Oh, my goodness. You are adorable!' She gazed up at Pippa with a full, open smile. 'What is his name?'

'Ginger. As in the hot and delicious gingerbread I'm hoping to eat while I'm back home.'

The woman threw her head back and chortled. She looked admiringly at Ginger as she ruffled Ginger's fur. 'Well, you certainly fit in well here at my cafe with a name like that.' She looked back up at Pippa. 'What made you decide to call him that? Is it his golden fur colour?'

'Hmm, not really. Although it suits him well now. He's named after Gingerbread. It was my mother's speciality. People came from far and wide to buy it at our pub.'

The woman gasped and stood up, pointing a finger at Pippa. 'Are you Brett's daughter?' Pippa nodded. 'Hello. I'm Katherine, the owner. We just missed out on meeting each other when I first opened this place. Your father said you'd just bought a place in Ireland.'

Pippa held her hand out. 'Yes, that's right. Hello Katherine. It's been a while since I was last here. You must have opened just after my last visit. My Aunt Morgan raves to me all the time about your herby sausage twists.'

Katherine laughed. 'When I make a batch, Morgan is my best customer. It's like she's got a six sense. She tells me they're all for Brett, but I swear she serves them up for breakfast to their hotel guests.'

Pippa's hand flew up to cover her open mouth and stifle a laugh. 'Oh no. That actually sounds like something my aunt would do, especially if the hotel was fully booked.' Pippa dropped her hand. 'Please let me extend my apologies. Although I'm certain Aunt Morgan wouldn't steal your thunder, I'm sure she'd tell the customers where they came from.'

A man in a baseball cap got up from his finished breakfast and walked up to the counter. He leaned his head close to Pippa's ear and talked out of the side of his mouth. 'Don't worry. Your secret apology is safe with me.'

Pippa swung her head around to see who the rude eavesdropping stranger was, but she was delighted to see it wasn't a stranger. It was her father's dear childhood friend.

'Ned.' She flung her arms around him and hugged him tight.

Ned hugged her back. 'Hello, Pip. I thought you were ignoring me. Then I realised you hadn't spotted me.'

Pippa flicked the brim of his cap. 'Of course I didn't see you with this on. Are you in disguise or something?'

Ned grabbed the rim of his cap and pulled it down, giving her a wink. 'It's the only way I can keep the swarms of local women at bay.' Katherine laughed and Ned winked at her.

Pippa shook her head with a smile. 'You haven't changed a bit, Ned.'

Ned grinned and looked towards Katherine. 'How much do I owe you, my dear?'

Katherine walked back behind the counter and looked down at a notepad. 'Four pounds and seventy-five pence please, Ned.'

Ned opened his wallet and withdrew a five-pound note. 'Put the change in the lifeboat rescue collection box.'

Pippa lovingly patted the side of his arm. 'You just can't stop giving to that job, can you, Ned?'

Ned shrugged. 'Just because I'm a retired lifeboat rescuer, it doesn't stop me from caring about the guys still working on the job... Talking of the guys, I'm off to pay them a visit. Give my regards to your Aunt Morgan when you see her will you, Pip?'

This time, Pippa winked. 'I'm sure you'll be able to give her your own regards when you see her yourself later on. Do you still call into the pub for your evening pint of Guinness?'

Ned nodded and smiled. 'Of course I do. It puts iron in my blood. But I've told you, your aunt and I are *just* very good friends.'

Pippa noticed Ned glance in Katherine's direction as he spoke. Ginger barked and started to whine again. Pippa crouched down beside him. 'Aww, sorry pup. Is your tummy rumbling?'

Ned ruffled the top of Ginger's head before making his way to the door, his hand raised in a farewell gesture. 'See you at the pub this evening, Pip.'

Pippa straightened and glanced over her shoulder. 'Yes. See you later, Ned.'

Katherine leaned her elbows on the countertop and looked down at Ginger then up to Pippa. 'Right, let's feed you two. What can I get you?'

Pippa smiled wryly. 'Got any of those famous herby sausage plaits?'

Katherine threw her head back and laughed.

***

An hour later, Pippa was turning her key in the side entrance door to the pub before quietly slipping inside. She wanted some alone time to say hello to the ghosts that haunted her before she saw her father. Once she'd had some time to herself in the pub, she'd go upstairs to the living quarters above the pub and make her presence known.

In the middle of the pub's lounge, Pippa unclipped Ginger's lead. He ran around, sniffing every seat, nook and cranny, his tail wagging frantically with happiness as he explored the residual aromas of the locals. Pippa smiled after him and wondered if he'd remembered any scents from the last time they were here. She set off to do her own exploring, dipping in and out of wonderful memories filled with her mother.

The pub's lounge room was much the same and Pippa smile shone on her face. The low beams of the ceiling were still stained black, the flagged stone tiles around the bar of the floor still had the same grooves, and the chairs and seats that ran around the edge of the walls were still covered in the deep sea-green velvet covering they'd been re-covered in five years ago—her mother's favourite colour. The only thing that was different was the drinking mats displaying a guest beer placed strategically on each wooden table top.

A clatter down in the cellar snapped her from her reveries, and Pippa looked around for her pooch. 'Ginger?' She quickly looked through the bar into the other room. But Ginger wasn't in the front bar room of the pub either. 'That little rascal. Someone must have left the door to the cellar open.'

Pippa walked over to the bar and sighed when she saw someone had indeed left the cellar door open. Her mouth downturned wondering if it was her father's doing, caused by his dementia. She carefully descended the steep stone steps. Halfway down, the cold of the underground basement room permeated her sweater and seeped into her bones. She shivered.

She'd always hated going into the cellar, and as a child tried her best to get out of it whenever her father had asked her to go down to fetch something. Most of the time she'd successfully bribed her brother with sweets to take her place. Even now the ghost rumours that were whispered by the locals terrified her, and even though she'd never actually witnessed any paranormal activities or apparitions in her entire life living there, her knuckles were still white outside her clenched fists.

Inside the cellar, Pippa crossed her arms over her chest and rubbed her hands up and down her upper arms. She opened her mouth to call out Ginger's name again, but she was too frightened to speak. Her eyes bugged out and swept from left to right as she walked further back in the enormous cellar.

She jumped out of her skin and then instantly became rigid with fear when something caught the corner of her eye. A white figure appeared at the back of the cellar in the shadows. Pippa was frozen to the spot—her feet rooted. Her body trembled slightly, but still, her feet wouldn't budge.

COMING HOME TO SEAGULL BAY 27

She couldn't move. But that didn't mean she had to look at the ghost. She squeezed her eyes together tightly and began to count in her head to distract herself from her terror. When she got to twenty, she forced herself to open them.

'Aarrrhhhh! Oliver. What on earth are you doing down here?'

Oliver was grinning down at her like a Cheshire cat. Pippa realised he was now wearing a cream padded ski jacket. He had only been wearing a blue pullover and jeans when he left the café earlier—not that she'd been paying his handsome face or his attire *that* much attention. He must have been the phantom figure she'd seen at the back of the cellar.

'Changing the barrels.'

Pippa's eyebrows shot up. 'What? Why?'

'I'm helping out at the pub for a bit. Your aunt Morgan asked my mother if I could.'

Pippa exhaled deeply as comprehension washed over her. Oliver was the son of the friend her aunt had mentioned in the letter. Pippa's stomach clenched with nervous excitement.

Ginger's bark at the top of the cellar's door made Pippa jump again. Oliver's hands curled around the tops of her arms. His touch made her arms tingle. 'Steady. Anyone would think you'd seen a ghost.' He finished the statement with a chuckle.

'Pippa? Is that you down there?'

Oliver released Pippa's arms, and she was surprised at how empty they instantly felt. She turned around and headed for the stairs. 'Yes, aunt Morgan. I was searching for Ginger.' At the bottom of the cellar steps, Pippa looked up and saw Ginger and her aunt looking down at her. Pippa's face lit up when she saw her aunt's lovely kind eyes. 'Aunt Morgan.' she squealed with delight and ran up the steps.

Her aunt held her arms open wide, her one hand still gripping her maple fish-headed walking stick. As soon as Pippa reached the top step, her aunt enveloped her in her arms, squeezing her with a vice-like grip she didn't know her aunt was capable of.

'When did you get here, my lovely?'

'About an hour ago.'

Footfall at the bottom of the stairs made her aunt pull away to look down into the cellar. Oliver waved up at them with a big, cheesy grin.

Aunt Morgan held Pippa at arm's length and looked from Oliver to Pippa with raised eyebrows. 'An hour, eh?'

Pippa was mortified by her aunt's innuendo, and pulled her away from the cellar doorway, past the bar, and towards the stairs up to the living quarters. 'Come on aunt. I'm gasping for a cup of tea. Is dad awake yet?'

'He's just in the shower, love.'

Pippa glanced back over her shoulder. 'Ginger! Come on, boy.'

Ginger ran between their legs and bounded up the stairs ahead of them. Pippa linked arms with her aunt and braced herself ready to be inundated with emotions and memories when she saw the multitude of photographs of her mother covering every square inch of the walls in the home she'd grown up in above the pub.

But when she walked into the lounge of her childhood home, most of the photographs had been removed. Pippa's jaw dropped as she looked from empty wall to empty wall.

Her aunt was at her side, squeezing her hand. 'I'm sorry, Pippa. I forgot to tell you in the letter that I'd had to take most of the photographs down. They were upsetting your father…Well, not exactly upsetting him, more overwhelming him.' She squeezed Pippa's hand a little harder. 'You do understand don't you, Kiddo?'

Pippa turned to look into her aunt's worried green eyes. She smiled through thin lips, barely able to contain her relief. Now, she could grieve for her mother in her own way without the constant sad reminder she was no longer there. 'Of course I don't mind, aunt. The house is exactly as it was when mom was alive. It's perfect.'

Aunt Morgan's shoulders appeared to visibly drop about two inches as she exhaled a relieved sigh.

The sitting room door clicked open and Pippa's father, Brett, came walking into the room whistling with a towel draped around his shoulders. He halted in his steps when he saw Pippa and stood motionless, staring at her. Pippa's heart all but stopped. Didn't he recognise her anymore? Then the corners of his mouth lifted from ear to ear.

'Pippa. My baby girl.'

Brett opened his arms wide and Pippa ran into them as she desperately tried to swallow past the lump in her throat whilst trying to stop the tears that had magically appeared again from falling.

'What are you doing here?'

Pippa's face was pressed against Brett's chest and her answer came out muffled. 'I've come to spend my annual leave here with you and aunt Morgan, maybe a bit longer. Is it okay if I stay in my old room this time, dad?'

Brett's arms squeezed her even tighter. 'Of course it is, my darling girl. Your mom will be over the moon.'

Pippa glanced over at aunt Morgan. Her aunt mouthed silently, 'Just a slip of the tongue,' and then she closed her eyes. Pippa noticed her nostrils flare and wondered if she was silently praying that was all it was.

Chapter three

An hour later, after spending some time with her father at the breakfast table catching up and getting the chance to assess his mental capacity herself, Pippa felt a lot more optimistic. Yet she was still slightly conflicted from her father's earlier comment about her mother being pleased to see her. Was it a slip of the tongue as her aunt had suggested?

Aunt Morgan had been right. There was no denying her father was a lot more forgetful than he'd been last time she'd been here to spend quality time with him, but he was nowhere near as bad as the image she'd conjured up in her mind of him either. Maybe this stay would turn out to be just annual leave length after all.

Aunt Morgan walked into the dining room from the kitchen and placed her teacup down onto its saucer before joining Brett and Pippa at the table. She cleared her throat and looked at Brett. 'Don't forget Brett, you have an appointment at the hospital at 1 PM today about your, erm...arthritis. I don't mind driving you to it. I know your arthritis flare up is giving you a lot of pain at the moment.'

Brett looked at aunt Morgan with a frown. 'Do I?' His eyebrows shot up when realisation dawned on him. 'Oh, I remember now. I should have written it on the calendar. Yes please Morgan, could you drive? My knees ache something rotten when I've been driving for more than an hour.'

Aunt Morgan turned to Pippa. 'You don't mind opening up today, do you, love? The cleaner has already been in to clean the pub and sort out the vacated hotel rooms, so you don't need to worry about them. All you need to do is open the pub, answer the phone for hotel bookings and possibly cook the odd lunch meal. Otherwise, just help Oliver behind the bar if it gets too busy. There is rarely anyone in for food at this time of the year, so it's not as if we're shoving you in at the deep end... Don't worry, your food hygiene certificate is still in date, I checked.'

Pippa opened and closed her mouth to reply before thinking better of it and opting for a sweet smile instead. She tilted her head to the side, giving her aunt a secret look oblivious to her father. 'That's lucky. Yes, of course I will. I've done it a thousand times before, so don't worry...I got this. I could run this place blindfolded.'

Brett nodded in agreement and turned to look at Morgan. 'She could you know, Morgan. Both Pippa and Nile ran the pub with ease for a few hours every week without us when they were in their late teens. Marie and I used to snatch an hour or two together on the beach.' Brett teared up. 'I do miss her you know, girls.'

Pippa jumped out of her seat and wrapped her arms around her father's neck, trying her hardest to keep her own tears at bay. 'I know, dad. We all do.' She looked across at her aunt, appealing for help with her eyes.

Morgan finished the last of her tea and stood up slowly, using her stick to help her. 'Right. That's me done. Are you almost ready, Brett? Once we hit the outskirts of the town and get on the main road, the traffic will be horrendous, so we are better off setting out early.'

Brett rubbed Pippa's arm lovingly and gave her a wink like he used to do when he playfully wound up her mother about something. Pippa smiled. 'Yes, Morgan. I'll just grab my hat and coat.'

Morgan reached for her bag. 'I've got your appointment letter in my handbag, so you don't need to worry about that. I'll meet you in the car.'

Pippa straightened and smiled her thanks to her aunt. 'Righto. I'd better make a start and get prepared for my first day back behind the bar.'

Brett stopped in his tracks and looked back over his shoulder at Pippa. 'Don't forget, Oliver will be here as well. It's Monday, so we'll probably only get the regulars, the retired folk, and maybe a couple of mothers with pushchairs and young children popping in for a spot of lunch and a catch up.'

Pippa walked over to Brett and squeezed her father's shoulders reassuringly. 'Don't worry. I told you, I got this. Why don't you and aunt Morgan stay in town and have a drink and a meal there? It will be a nice treat, and it will be a chance to check out what the urban pubs are doing, food wise.'

Her aunt smiled. 'Good idea Pippa. I'd love that.' She turned to look at her brother-in-law. 'Brett, what do you say?'

Brett looked at Morgan and nodded. 'Yes, I don't mind checking out a rival's beer...or two.'

Ginger got up from the plush rug Aunt Morgan had laid down for him and barked. Pippa ruffled his head. 'What is it, boy? Can you hear the post being delivered?'

'It's probably Oliver. I gave him the spare key while he's helping out,' said Aunt Morgan. 'He usually pops over to Katherine's café and grabs some breakfast before he starts.'

Pippa's mouth dropped open. 'Oh, I forgot he was helping out.'

Aunt Morgan smiled. 'Is there anything we should know about? Any skeletons in the closet between you two?'

Pippa shook her head. 'Goodness, no. You probably don't remember, but I was close to him at school for a short period...that's all.' Pippa finished her sentence with a shrug. Brett was still facing Morgan, so she walked up to him and placed a hand on her father's shoulder and squeezed. He reached up and patted it. 'I'll see you later, dad. Just relax and have a nice day with Aunt Morgan. The pub will be fine.' She looked around at Ginger and slapped her thigh before heading to the door leading out to the stairs. 'Come on, boy.'

***

Oliver was already taking the stools off the tables and placing them on the floor, left there after the cleaner had vacuumed and moped earlier in the morning. Ginger bounded over to him and immediately started sniffing at the ankles of his jeans. Oliver crouched down and ruffled the fur at Ginger's neck with both of his hands. 'Hello again. Can you smell my Jess, boy?'

'Ginger.'

Oliver looked up with a smile and shook his head. 'No, thank you. I've already eaten. Anyway, it's a bit early for Ginger—*bread or biscuits*. I prefer a more savoury breakfast myself.' Pippa chuckled. Oliver drew his eyebrows together, acting dumb. 'What's so funny?'

Pippa shook her head. 'No silly. My dog is named Ginger.'

Oliver winked, before joining in with the laughter. His laughter turned into a smile. 'Morning Pippa. I knew you were addressing Ginger. I was just fooling with you. Although it's funny how names can change the trajectory of one's life, isn't it?'

Pippa frowned. 'How do you mean?'

'Well, take the singer, *Cat Stevens* for instance. He started off as a singer songwriter, but then he changed his name to Yusuf Islam, which took him on a slightly different life journey.'

Pippa nodded. 'Yes, I guess that's a good example.' She made a move to walk towards the bar entrance.

Oliver followed her. 'What I'm trying to do Pippa, is to explain why I broke up with you all those years ago.' Pippa stopped in her tracks and stiffened. She couldn't believe he was bringing that up now, especially as they were about to spend a whole day working together.

She turned to face him and shook her head. 'It really doesn't matter, Oliver...we were just teenagers.' Her stomach had clenched into a tight knot. She *did* want to know. It had eaten away at her for years, but what if she didn't like the answer?

She had spent months—*years even*—analysing their break-up, wondering if it had been a physical attribute that had suddenly made him break up with her back then when they were adolescents. What had he disliked about her? Yes, she desperately wanted to know the reason for him dumping her. It was a teenage girl's prerogative, after all to know such things.

But what if she didn't like his answer? What if he were to tell her she had been too short? Too spotty? That it was it her brace or the size of her nostrils that had been the reason for their break-up?

If he were to blame her physical appearance back then as the reason, she couldn't promise her reaction wouldn't be to punch him on the end of the nose—even though she was averse to violence. Then where would that leave them?

'Pippa Pickles and Oliver Onions is what everyone was whispering behind our backs,' Oliver blurted out.

Pippa was gobsmacked. 'What?'

'At school...that is what everyone was calling us when we dated... But not only that, they said when we got married we'd have pickled onion smelling babies.'

The laugh that spluttered from Pippa's mouth was one of disbelief and surprise. 'I-I never heard anyone call us those horrid names. My friends would have told me... I get why they'd want to call *me* pickles. The pub is after all called The Cheese Wedge and Pickles, so Pippa Pickles was quite predictable, I suppose. But Oliver Onions? Were they paying reference to you dating a girl they nicknamed Pickle?'

'I think it was partly that, and also because of my surname...Oney.'

Pippa gasped and her hands flew up to her cheeks. 'Blimey. Kids can be so cruel, can't they?' She fixed Oliver with a stare. 'So you dumped me without explanation because of a bit of name calling going on behind our backs? I would have appreciated an explanation instead of just dropping me like a ton of bricks and ignoring me, Ollie.'

His features softened. 'You haven't called me that for a long time.' Oliver bit his bottom lip and searched Pippa's eyes. 'That's why I'm telling you now, Pippa. I've wanted to apologise for so long. Believe it or not, the awful way I'd dumped you plagued me for years. When I was living in America with my dad, I even sought out the pub's number and called it to apologise to you. But whoever answered told me you were away at uni.'

Pippa's stomach was clenched so tight it was starting to hurt. She waved her hand dismissively and turned away to hide the burning red of her cheeks. 'It's all water under the bridge now. I think we should just forget about it. That was a lifetime ago. Let's just get to work.' She walked over to the bar and headed for the door next to it into the sanctuary of the kitchen to check the stock.

Oliver called after her. 'Does that mean I'm forgiven?'

She didn't answer. She was trembling. All these years of not knowing why he had dumped her and it had been over something as trivial as *that*.

***

They worked side by side, preparing to open the pub in relative silence, with just the occasional glace thrown in both directions.

Oliver was the first to speak. 'Shall I man the bar and you manage the phone bookings and kitchen?'

Pippa stopped what she was doing and raised an eyebrow. 'Is that because I'm a woman?'

Oliver's face blanched, and he shook his head quickly. 'No. Not at all. I just thought because of your dislike of going into the cellar I'd work the bar—in case a barrel needed changing. I know the Guinness is low because Ned and his retired boat rescue buddies gave it a hammering the night before last.'

Pippa hid her surprise. He'd actually remembered her fear of the basement. She shrugged. 'Fine.'

Oliver returned the gesture. 'Fine.'

She watched him as he walked over to the main door to open up. He must have grown another four inches when he left high school. Now he was six foot two, at least. His shirt pulled tight on his broad shoulders as he reached to unbolt the dead lock.

Pippa's chest fluttered. She sucked in a breath and sighed. Yes, he certainly was the one who got away. But maybe that was a good thing. If he couldn't defend her honour by putting an end to the name calling behind her back when they were dating, what good would he have been as husband material?

He turned to face her, and she felt her cheeks burn again at being caught staring at him. But she couldn't help it. Pippa had found herself staring at him all morning whenever she'd had a chance.

She'd been pleasantly surprised by how immaculately turned out he'd been when he'd come back to the pub after she'd seen him earlier that morning, first in the cafe and then in the cellar. Now his beard and moustache were neatly trimmed and he was wearing a shirt and tie with *nice* jeans—very possibly designer ones, matched with lovely brown dress shoes. His hair was still a little on the long side, a wavy mess, but it only added to his rugged charm. She hated that her stomach did a loop the loop every time he walked past her and she caught scent of his cologne, expensive like his jeans.

Pippa was just about to turn around and head into the kitchen when a large group of ramblers jostled in as soon as the doors were opened.

The man in front of the group dipped his head at Oliver and then looked across to Pippa as he led the way. 'Good afternoon. What a wonderful morning we've had.'

Pippa smiled. 'Good afternoon.'

Oliver hurried ahead of the group and slipped behind the bar. 'Good afternoon. Where have you been hiking?'

'We've walked along the permissive footpaths over the farmers' fields from the neighbouring village where we've been staying for a couple of nights in their bed-and-breakfast. The B & B owner informed us that The Cheese Wedge and Pickles pub in the next village is also a hotel, so we thought we'd make this our final destination of the day and see if we could get booked in for a few days. I've looked on the map and there are lots of wonderful walks we'd like to do around here.'

Oliver turned to Pippa with raised eyebrows. Pippa looked from the rambler to Oliver before she realised he was waiting for her reply. 'Oh...right. Let me just check the bookings while Oliver takes your bar orders.' She returned the raised eyebrow gesture to him before turning around and walking over to the hotel bookings book.

Oliver cleared his throat behind her. 'Right, ladies and gentlemen. What can I get for you?'

'Can we open a tab?'

'Yes, of course,' nodded Oliver. There was an influx of orders fired at Oliver and Pippa smiled to herself as she listened to him getting flustered. She opened the bookings book and turned to today's date.

The party of ramblers was in luck. All the rooms except one were free until the following weekend. Pippa turned around with a bright smile, made even bigger when she saw Oliver attempting to multi-task, which didn't appear to be going very well.

'We have three double rooms and four single rooms available. One of the double rooms has twin beds in it. How many would you like to book?'

The hiker looked perplexed. 'Oh. There's actually eleven of us.'

Pippa remembered the spare cot bed that was on wheels. 'I can add a single bed to one of the rooms. It's no problem if that's okay with your friends.'

A few of the heads nodded. 'Perfect,' smiled the hiker. 'Is it also possible to order lunch and an evening meal?'

Oliver glanced at Pippa as he juggled pouring two drinks and grinned smugly.

Pippa ignored his grin. 'Erm. Yes, of course.' She grabbed a handful of lunch menus and handed them to the hiker. 'The evening meal menu will be available for you to peruse after 4 PM. We have to wait to see what local produce is available before the menu is decided.' Oliver swiped a surprised glance Pippa's way at her comment.

The hiker took the menus and passed them out to the ramblers who had been served by Oliver. They made their way over to a group of tables nestled by the open fire Oliver had stoked before Pippa had come down that morning.

When they were all served and seated studying the menus, Oliver dabbed at his brow and breathed out from puffed up cheeks. 'Wow, I wasn't expecting that.' He turned to look at Pippa. 'What was all that about local produce?'

Pippa chewed on her lower lip in thought before answering. 'We have hardly any fresh supplies in. As soon as we close, I'm going to have to call on Ben the fisherman, and then the farm shop. I know in the past we've always gotten our supplies from them and as far as I'm aware, nothing has changed. But if business is on the turn and getting busier, I might suggest to dad we hire a chef sooner rather than later if we're starting to get passing trade like this.'

Pippa was surprised when, without warning, Oliver reached up and pushed a strand of hair off her face. 'Let me know if you need any help.'

She could feel mini volcanos erupting underneath her cheeks again as her capillaries popped. 'I-I think I'll manage.' She spun on her heels and headed for the door to the kitchen, her heart beating a lot faster than it had done a minute earlier.

Chapter four

Pippa kicked off her shoes, sank into the sofa, and put her feet up on the coffee table. Ginger jumped onto her lap and she let out a surprised yelp. 'Crikey, Ginger. You're getting heavy. I think both you and I could benefit from a good hike ourselves. Just let me have ten minute's rest boy and then we'll get the food supplies for this evening.' Ginger licked at Pippa's cheek.

A knock on the sitting-room door made Pippa jump with a start, which set Ginger off, barking. She quickly dropped her feet down and sat up poker straight. 'Who is it?'

Oliver's face peered around the door. 'I'm just letting you know I've put the spare bed in the hotel room, and I'm off now.'

Pippa's hand flew to her forehead. 'Oh, I'd completely forgotten about that. Thank you, Oliver.'

Oliver nodded with a smile, which quickly turned into a frown. 'You have a little something—' He pointed to Pippa's face.

Pippa dropped her hand and started to rub at the place Oliver was gesturing at. He shook his head. 'No...there.'

'Where? What is it?' She was mortified. She probably looked a right state after her marathon cooking session. It's not as if she was used to cooking for more than one lately.

Oliver pushed past the crack in the door and strode towards her. Ginger jumped up onto Pippa's knees, wagging his tail. 'Ow, you big lump. You're digging your claws into me. You definitely need to go for a walk.'

Oliver stroked Ginger and then knelt on one knee in front of Pippa. It was exactly the position the faceless man who

42

proposed to her countless times in her dreams got into. He raised his hand and gently rubbed at something on the end of her nose. This time there was nowhere to escape to hide the crimson colour instantly staining her cheeks. Her heart hammered in her chest.

'Erm, thanks.'

Oliver's eyes seemed to linger a little too long on her before he peeled them away to look at Ginger as he stroked both his ears simultaneously. 'Would you like to meet Jess, my girl?' Pippa felt a pang of envy, thinking Oliver meant his girlfriend before she remembered Jess was Oliver's pet Labrador. He looked back at Pippa. 'What do you say, Pippa?'

'Huh?'

'You and I? Taking our dogs on a date?'

'A date?' Her heart drummed harder.

'Yes. We could introduce our pets. It would be like a doggy date. We could take them on a walk together.'

'Ohhh...right. Yes, we could see if they got along with each other. Ginger hasn't had a very good social life in Ireland, but he has been friendly with the few dogs he's met.'

Oliver held her eyes with a penetrating stare and a smile that could melt a thousand single ladies' hearts. 'And what about Ginger's owner? Has she had a good social life?'

Pippa forced out a smile. She didn't want Oliver, a man she dated briefly in high-school and hadn't seen for years knowing her social life was all but non-existent since her mother's passing. Apart from the odd lunch date with her new Irish girlfriends, she had locked herself away in her apartment and let work consume her. She hadn't even met up with her childhood friends still living in the village yet.

'Ginger's owner doesn't do too badly,' she *white* lied.

Pippa noticed Oliver's smile falter. He quickly got back up on his feet. 'Right. I'd better get off. I have a ton of work to catch up with, and I'm expecting a call from America.'

Ginger jumped down from Pippa's legs and bounded over to the door. Pippa stood up too. 'Of course. Aunt Morgan mentioned you were only helping out for a short while because you had your own business to attend to. What is it you do?'

'I'm a web designer. I'm lucky, I can work from any location and work hours to suit myself. I must admit though, I'm loving the change-up of working here. Working in a pub has always been a secret desire of mine. Well, to be precise. I've had a desire to work in *this* pub.' Pippa smiled. He pointed at her chest. 'You're in marketing, aren't you, Pippa?' Pippa's eyebrows rose. She was surprised he knew. Oliver was quick to offer the reason he knew. 'Your aunt Morgan was telling me about a contract you were working on when I mentioned the pub should update their website and do some marketing to promote it.'

Pippa nibbled on her bottom lip and looked thoughtful. 'Yes, the pub's website does need jollying up. Maybe you could offer your suggestions on how we can improve it when we go on that date.' Oliver's eyes widened. 'The *doggy* date,' she reminded him.

'Ah, right...of course. Yes. I'll be happy to make suggestions.'

They stood motionless for a moment in silence, staring at each other. When Oliver made no attempt to leave, Pippa clapped her hands together, breaking the sizzling tension zinging back and forth between them. 'Right. I must crack on. I have to purchase the supplies to feed the ramblers.'

Oliver shuffled on the spot before nodding and turning to leave. He walked over to the door and glanced back before he walked through it. 'See you later.'

'Yes. See you later.'

Pippa sighed when he was gone. Thankfully, he'd taken the crackling tension between them with him.

***

It had been an age since she'd been to purchase supplies from the local traders. The last time had been with her mother when they'd been fully booked for Christmas lunches four years ago. How they'd laughed when the large bag of sprouts her mother had been carrying from the car into the pub had ripped open in the lounge, spilling mini green bombs everywhere. The cleaner had complained of finding the odd sprout, right up until Valentine's day.

Instead of the usual bucket-load of tears she usually shed when she thought about her mother, this time the memory left her with a beaming smile and warmth enveloping her heart. It was a wonderful experience and Pippa felt as if her heart had healed just a sliver.

First she visited Ben the local fisherman at his small fishmonger business, which he ran out of a wooden hut at the side of his house. She smelt the fresh fish before she raised her fist to knock on his hut door. Ben opened the door with curious eyes that crinkled up at the corners when he recognised Pippa.

'Well, I'll be blown over in a hurricane. If it isn't little Pippa from the pub.'

Pippa gave him a toothy grin. Ben hadn't changed a bit. He still chewed on a wooden toothpick angled out of the side of his mouth. A toothpick had been a permanent fixture in his mouth for as long as Pippa could remember. His scraggy grey beard was much the same as when she was a little girl and the only difference she noted from his appearance from the last time she'd seen him, was he was now wearing a red woollen hat instead of a navy one, the colour of the hat she'd seen him wear the last time she'd been there with her mother.

'I'm not so little now and I wasn't so little the last time I saw you either, Ben.'

He waved her words away with the flick of a very wrinkled and veiny hand. 'Bah, you'll always be little to me, girl.' He turned his back on her and hobbled over to a stool next to a chest freezer and pulled up the knees of his dungarees before he sat down. 'You've missed the day's catch. Alls that's left is the fish I didn't sell, which I've frozen.'

'That's fine, Ben. I've got a group booking I wasn't expecting, so beggars can't be choosers, eh?'

He nodded with a chuckle. 'Where's your pop? Is he being lazy and sending you to do his dirty work?'

Pippa laughed. 'No. He had an appointment and Aunt Morgan drove him to it because his arthritis has flared up again. They planned to stop in the city for a bite to eat before they came back. Actually, Ben. I'll probably be coming to get supplies most mornings for the next couple of weeks...maybe longer.'

Pippa's comment appeared to pique Ben's curiosity. 'Oh ay? Are you planning on moving back, lass?'

Pippa shrugged. 'Maybe.'

'How come?'

Pippa grinned. 'Because I've missed your ragged, old, handsome face, that's why.'

Ben howled with laughter. 'Hey, less of the old.' He lifted the lid of the chest freezer. 'What you 'avin then, lass?'

'Just give me two dozen of whatever you have. Some of the guests might not be fish eaters, but I need to make sure I have the supply to meet the demand if I get more bookings.'

'Got an icebox?'

Pippa lifted what she was carrying. 'I sure do.'

***

Her next stop was the farm. Everything there was organic. It was a little pricy for the general public, but there was no arguing against the quality. Pippa had to slow her car to a total stop to let a herd of cows roam lazily across the dirt road as she made her way to the farm shop.

Big clouds of steam billowed from the cows' wet nostrils in the cold spring air. Pippa shivered. She had the car heater turned all the way up, but the cows appeared to be oblivious to the low temperature outside. The sky was full of dark white clouds, either threatening a downfall of snow or rain. Soon, Phil, the owner of the farm and his son Pharis would bed the cows down for the night.

Pippa spotted Pharis and lowered the window of her car to poke out her arm and wave. She didn't want to chance scaring the cows with the car horn. 'Hey, Pharis!' He waved back.

Pippa had known Pharis since they were really young. Best friends with her younger brother, Nile. He'd been a frequent visitor in their pub and home since childhood—especially when Nile and Pharis became teenagers. Pippa suspected they pulled themselves the odd sneaky pint of beer when they thought no one was looking, although she could never prove it. Pharis had been gutted when her brother had enlisted in the paratroopers and he'd been like a lost sheep ever since.

He walked towards her car, shooing the cows out of his way. 'Pippa. Wow, it's been ages since you've been back home. It's really good to see you again.'

'It's great to see you too, Pharis. How are things? How are your parents?'

'Mom and dad are great. The farm is doing well. But I'm bored. I can't wait for Nile to come home on leave again.'

'When is his next leave?' asked Pippa.

Pharis laughed. 'You're his sister. You should know.'

'We might be siblings, but your bond is thicker with Nile than mine is. You two were always inseparable. I'm surprised when you didn't enlist with him.'

Pharis shook his head slowly with pursed lips. 'Believe me, if I hadn't have been an only child I would have, but mom and dad needed me.'

Pippa nodded in agreement. 'So do I. I need you to help me restock the pub's pantry. We have eleven guests and I have no idea how long they are staying. It could be one night it might be four.'

Pharis tapped the roof of the mini and pointed over to the farm shop. 'Pull up over there, Pippa, and I'll see what deal I can do for you.' Pippa nodded and raised her window. The farm shop looked more like a designer shed with panelled wooden slats vertically cladding the exterior walls. It had a string of white lights along the edge of the roof, which became multi-coloured over the Christmas holiday and orange at Halloween when there was an abundance of pumpkins to sell. Inside was like an Aladdin's cave with wooden handmade toys supplied by a local toy maker alongside the produce. It was a child's delight and a parent's nightmare if all they wanted to buy was food.

Pharis reached the farm shop just as she was climbing out of her car. 'I've just remembered. There's a surprise in the shop for you, Pippa.'

Pippa closed the car door and turned to him with a grin. 'Really? What is it?'

Pharis smiled and motioned for her to follow him. 'Come in and you'll see.'

Pippa followed Pharis into the shop with a little flutter of excitement in her stomach. There was a young girl about eighteen sitting behind the till who looked up and smiled when they walked into the shop, but there were no other customers, which wasn't surprising, as it was early closing that day. Pippa was thankful the shop was still open and that she'd made it. She silently scolded herself for taking so long to come and get her supplies. By the time she headed back to the pub, there would only be an hour or so to decide what was on this evening's menu and prepare the food. Tonight, she would definitely need help in the kitchen.

Pippa stopped in her tracks when she saw what the surprise was. Right at the back of the shop was a poster at least ten feet tall and six feet wide, advertising the farm's home-grown organic beef. The background picture was a scene of the town's annual bar-b-q from four years ago, and right in the centre next to Pharis's parents was Marie, Pippa's mother, with her head back laughing.

Pippa froze. Up until then, any picture hung on a wall had made her instantly tear up, but this picture reflected that perfect moment from her mother's last summer alive. It was the epitome of balmy summer happiness.

'Wow...just *wow*. You do realise I'll be in here almost every day now Pharis, just to look at that wonderful poster.'

'No need. I have a smaller version just for you.' Pharis walked behind the counter and fished out a cardboard cylinder and handed it to Pippa.

Pippa took it and held it close to her heart. 'Thank you, Pharis. I'll treasure it.'

Pharis nodded with a small understanding smile and then clapped his hands together. 'Okay. What do you want because I need to shut up shop? I have a wonderful home-cooked beef stew waiting for me, curtesy of my Ma.'

It wasn't until Pippa was in the car and driving back down the lane did she let the tears fall.

Chapter five

Back at the pub and in the kitchen, Pippa was running from one thing to the other, frantically trying to prepare the meals the ramblers had pre-ordered after an anxious re-hashing of the current menu on her laptop and printing them off when she'd returned from the farm.

She was already exhausted, and it was only the start of the evening shift. Vegetables and potatoes were bubbling away, filling the kitchen with steam, and the mixed aroma of fish and meat pasties filled the air.

Oliver walked into the kitchen, but Pippa hadn't even noticed he was there, slamming into his chest as she turned around. 'Oh sorry, Ollie.' She noticed his mouth quirk at the use of the abbreviated nickname she'd given him while they were dating at school. 'Have you come to help?' She blew upwards out of the side of her mouth because her hands were covered in flour, trying unsuccessfully to move a stray strand of hair attached to one of her eyelashes, after having escaped the clip she'd used to pile her unruly curls on top of her head.

'Allow me.' Oliver tucked the strand of hair over her ear. The heat she'd experienced numerous times today whenever she was around Oliver exploded underneath her cheeks again, but she was already hot and bothered, so she was sure Oliver wouldn't even notice. 'I wished I could, Pippa, but all the locals have piled in too.' He grimaced, 'I've just come to tell you, we have another two orders for pasties, potatoes, gravy and veg.' Pippa audibly sighed. 'When do you think Brett and Morgan will be back?'

Pippa shook her head, 'I honestly don't know Oliver, but if the food side of the business continuous to grow like this, they will need to hire a proper chef.'

'*Oliver*!'

Oliver looked over his shoulder, back towards the way he'd come in. One of the locals was calling for service. He placed a hand on Pippa's shoulder. 'I'd better get back.' He squeezed it. 'Come on. We can get through this...together.'

'*Service*!'

A different voice called out from the bar. Pippa grimaced. 'You'd better get back. Just discourage them from ordering any more food.'

Oliver laughed. 'Shall I tell them the beer pumps have dried up, too?' He smiled a dazzling smile and the stresses of the kitchen instantly vanished. 'Nice try, Pippa Pickles.'

'Hey!' Pippa laughed. 'It's Pippa Bramwell, as you rightly know. Don't reignite the use of that ghastly name the kids at school *apparently* called me, or I might just have to start addressing you as Ollie Onions.'

'Touché. Sorry. That was a little tactless of me. Especially as it was the catalyst of our break-up.'

Pippa lifted her eyebrows at his comment and stared directly into the brown pools of his eyes, but instantly regretted it, as she was now drowning in them. She blinked to snap out of the trance they'd cast over her. 'No. I'd say that was down to you alone.' Oliver looked taken aback. Pippa turned her back on him dismissively. The stab of hurt from the mention of the break-up followed by the sizzling attraction she'd just felt had taken her by surprise. They were young when they'd dated. It's not as if Oliver had been *the one*...or had he? 'You'd better get back.'

'Yes, I better *had*.' Pippa couldn't see his face, but she knew exactly how he'd look from the curt tone of his reply. She'd hit a nerve...good.

The rest of the evening flew by. There were more food orders, but no more conversation between them when Oliver came into the kitchen to deliver the orders. In fact, Pippa noticed he barely even looked her in the eye. She was glad. It was hard enough concentrating on cooking without the added distraction from him, his dashing good looks, and his *not* so clever comments.

When it was five minutes to the cut-off time for food orders, and the door to the kitchen opened again, Pippa was seriously considering telling Oliver to go away in a not so very polite manner. But when she turned around, to her relief, it was her aunt Morgan and not him.

'Crikey! Have you brought fairy dust with you? Where did all those people come from? You've even attracted locals we usually only see on special occasions such as Christmas.'

Pippa's shoulders dropped with relief when she realised her aunt wasn't here to issue her with another food order. 'Oh, Aunt Morgan. What a day. I forgot how much there was to do. I'm used to sitting behind my laptop all day, with the only body parts moving being my fingers.'

Aunt Morgan laughed and walked over to Pippa, pulling her into her arms for a hug. 'You've done amazingly well—both you and Oliver. But more so you, because in my opinion, being the cook is the tougher of the two roles. Plus, you've had to act as server too.'

Pippa sighed heavily into her aunt's shoulder. 'You're not kidding.' She pulled away and looked at her through tired eyes. 'Anyway, how did the appointment go? I'm guessing by your body language this morning it wasn't really for his arthritis.'

Aunt Morgan gave Pippa a small smile. 'It wasn't all doom and gloom. The consultant was actually very pleased with the limited progression of the disease. He said the tablets he'd prescribed to slow it down are doing their job. He did however mention it might be beneficial if Brett were to go to a memory clinic, a weekly one, even possibly a weekend one too. That would mean missing some of the lunchtime business hours, but you already know you're here to help out while I persuade him to sell up. However, if it continues to be busy like this, until the business is on the market, I think we need to hire a chef again as soon as possible. Otherwise, you'll be returning to Ireland, needing a holiday to get over your visit here.'

Pippa sighed and smiled. 'Thank goodness the dementia hasn't progressed any more. I've been a bag of nerves since I received your letter.'

Aunt Morgan pulled Pippa in for another hug. 'I'm sorry for the distress I've caused you, Kiddo.'

'It's not your fault, aunt.' She pulled away to look her in the eyes. 'I'm glad you made me come…I really am. I'm just sorry it's taken so long for me to come back. I bet you thought I've been heartless staying away for so long. Especially as it's only been three years since mom's passing.'

Aunt Morgan shook her head. 'Not at all, my darling. We all deal with grief in different ways. It was obviously too raw for you to be here.'

'It was with all the photos dad hung up on the walls straight after the funeral, aunt.' Pippa blurted out. 'It was just too much...a constant reminder I'd lost one of the most important people in the world to me.'

Aunt Morgan rubbed her hand up and down the top of Pippa's arm. 'I did wonder about them when Brett hung them up. But then, that was his way of coping with grief.'

Pippa nodded. 'I know, Aunt. I just wish I could have manned up and been here more for dad. Especially now, knowing of his dementia.'

'Hey, don't beat yourself up, Kiddo... At your father's request, he doesn't want you to know about it, remember? Anyway, you are here now, so that's all that counts.' Pippa sighed again and nodded. 'You look exhausted, Pippa. Have you and Oliver eaten yet?'

'I haven't. I'm not sure if Oliver ate before he came to work.'

'Go and sit at the bar. I'll clean up here and rustle up something for both of you.'

'But your MS, aunt.'

Aunt Morgan gave Pippa a small smile. 'At times I might be slightly impaired physically, but that doesn't mean I can't look after my wonderful niece when she needs it. Now go...do as you are told.' She ended the sentence with a bigger smile as she pointed to the kitchen door with her walking stick.

Pippa partly grimaced and partly smiled. 'Yes, Aunt.'

Her father was behind the bar counter, pulling a pint, and Oliver was sitting at the bar on the customer's side when Pippa entered the pub lounge. Pippa raised her eyebrows questioningly as she approached.

Oliver gestured towards her father. 'He literally ordered me to sit down and take a break.'

A huge smile brightened Pippa's face. 'Yep, that's my dad.'

Brett was laughing and joking with a couple of the ramblers, a king in his castle. Pippa settled onto the bar stool next to Oliver and then both watched Brett in awe. He was the perfect host. Laughing along with his new customers and charming them as he regaled the ramblers with tales of his afternoon in the city, sampling beers from popular pubs.

'We did okay, didn't we?'

Pippa turned away from watching her father and looked at Oliver. He had been studying her profile.

She smiled at him coyly. 'We did. But that was just round one of many for me.'

Oliver looked surprised. 'Do you intend staying here a long time?'

Pippa didn't want to give too much away. 'I only intended to stay a week, maybe two. But my aunt and dad haven't really had any time off since my mom's passing, so I thought I'd stick around a little longer. Maybe extend my visit for at least a month, maybe more.'

Oliver nodded and looked deep in contemplation. 'I told Morgan I'd help out until Brett's arthritis flare up calmed down, but if it stays busy like this, I don't mind extending my help, too. I can always catch up with my own business in my free time.'

A flurry of butterflies raced around Pippa's stomach. It would be nice to spend more time with Oliver and catch up on the years apart. 'Won't your business suffer though?'

Oliver shrugged. 'I don't really know, but the crazy thing is...I don't really care. I'm loving it working here. As you know, I've always wanted to work behind that bar.' He pointed to where Brett stood. 'I always had it in my head at high school that once I'd finished uni. I'd nab the first part-time job that became available here, whilst I applied for apprentice positions in tech companies.' He suddenly looked miles away. 'But who'd have thought my life would be turned upside down by my parent's divorce? Taking me on a different path, and moving me away from here to the US?'

Brett leaned on the pumps towards them. 'What can I get for the workers?'

Pippa gasped and stuck out her tongue, fawning dehydration. 'I'm parched, dad. Can I have a pint of soda water and lime, please?'

'Not a glass of Guinness?' Brett looked surprised.

'Maybe later. A half pint at last orders.'

Brett turned his head and looked at Oliver. 'Oliver?'

Oliver grinned. 'It depends on if I'm coming back behind the bar tonight?'

Brett laughed, and the deep, hearty tones of his voice drew smiles from the locals. 'Looks like you're in good spirits tonight, Brett.' called out Ned, his hand hovering mid-air ready to take his shot at the dartboard.

'I am, Ned. I've got my daughter back.'

Pippa's heart felt as though it had swollen to twice its size. She had to take in a long, deep breath to stop herself from welling up.

Brett drew his attention back to Oliver. 'You don't need to work the bar anymore tonight, Oliver. I'm feeling on top of the world. My arthritis pain has been better all day, but that's not to say it won't give me jip tomorrow. But while I'm pain free, I'm happy to be standing here on this side of the bar. Why don't you stay where you are and keep my lovely daughter company?'

Pippa's stomach clenched tight. Any other time she'd be happy at the suggestion, but after working in the kitchen all night she knew she looked a mess, and probably stank of cooking, too. 'I-I'm only staying down here for another half an hour, dad. I need to see to Ginger. He's still upstairs and he'll need to be let out to pee.'

Brett frowned. 'You can bring him in here after you've seen to him, love. We are a dog-friendly pub, or has it been so long since you've been here, you've forgotten?'

Pippa's mouth dropped open just as Morgan appeared with a tray of tapas style foods she'd made up from the cooked leftovers Pippa had kept warm in the oven. Aunt Morgan set them down on the bar in front of Pippa and Oliver. 'There you go. You two don't mind sharing this lot, do you? Of course, I've brought out two forks and two plates, so just help yourselves.'

Oliver beamed. 'Wow. Thank you, Morgan. This looks amazing.'

'Don't thank me. I didn't cook it. It was Pippa. I'm taking no credit. I'm going to make a start cleaning up the kitchen while you tuck in.'

Pippa stood up. 'I'll do it aunt.'

'No. You sit down and eat your supper. You've both worked really hard today while Brett and I have been off gallivanting. It's time for us to roll up our sleeves and do a bit of work now.'

Pippa plonked herself back down on the seat with a small sigh and a smile. 'Thanks Aunt.'

COMING HOME TO SEAGULL BAY 59

Oliver scooped a bit of everything onto his plate and tucked in. He made appreciative noises and Pippa glanced at him with a grin, feeling quite pleased with herself. She was a decent cook, but she wasn't about to win any a la carte competitions.

'Mmm, very nice.'

'Aunt Morgan must have added magic spices to what I already cooked because I didn't make anything special.' She took a bite of her own cooking. It didn't taste as if it had been altered and she was surprised by how good it was. She had been in too much of a dither to appreciate it when she'd sampled it earlier, before she'd plated it up for the evening's diners. She was pleased Oliver was enjoying it.

'I'd love to see Ginger again. Will you bring him in here after you've eaten? I'll save him a piece of meat.'

Pippa looked around the busy pub at the customers. Some were regulars she hadn't spoken to in ages. She *did* need to do the rounds and catch up. The rest were the ramblers who were staying at the hotel, which was attached to the back of the pub. She hadn't intended staying down here for the remainder of the evening, but Pippa thought it would be nice to catch up with old friends from the community, plus Ginger would adore the attention. 'Yes, why not?' Her answer seemed to please Oliver because his face brightened considerably.

They sat side by side in silence as they ate and listened to Brett continue to entertain a couple of ramblers sitting at the other end of the bar, telling them tales about how the village used to hold maypole dancing at the annual fete, amongst other things, up until there was a period in the village when there were not enough volunteers so it just naturally came to an end.

Oliver turned to Pippa. 'It's so sad. I remember my mother telling me about all the community gatherings coming to an end in a telephone conversation when I was living with my father in the US. This town needs to do all of those fantastic things again and bring the old traditions back so the younger generations get to enjoy them as much as we did. There are more and more traditions being lost these days.'

Pippa nodded. 'I agree. I was at uni when the maypole dancing stopped. I also remember my mother telling me she and a couple of other people were trying to get volunteers, but there just weren't enough.' The thought of her mother rallying the community as she always used to make her chest tighten. She felt fiercely proud of her, yet so very sad.

Oliver placed his hand on top of hers, which was resting on the bar. 'Are you alright, Pippa?'

Pippa drew in an astonished gasp and quickly pulled it away, dropping it into her lap. She pushed away her sad face and plastered a smile on her lips, which didn't reach her eyes as she nodded a little too eagerly. 'Yes, I'm experiencing a touch of nostalgia is all.' She stood up. 'I-I think I'll call it a night. I'll see you next time you're here, Oliver.'

Without waiting for an answer, she turned on her heels and headed for the door, which would take her out to the stairs leading up to the living quarters above the pub.

Nodding her head to acknowledge faces she recognised as they turned towards her as she passed them, she said her hellos, made promises to catch up another time, and then her goodnights. But as she reached the door, the eyes she felt burning into the back of her head belonged to none other than Oliver.

Act – 2 Chapter six

The sea water shimmered, looking too beautiful in Pippa's opinion for such a cold morning. She shivered as a breeze parted the hair at the nape of her neck and blew down the back of her scarf, raising goosebumps across her skin. She shivered and pulled it tighter around her neck, then dug her hands into the deep pockets of her woollen duffel coat.

Ginger raced through the frothy waves lashing at his legs oblivious to the low temperature, his tail wagged furiously, showing his ecstasy at being in the natural environment.

Pippa's tummy pinched with a pang of guilt. He got nowhere enough exercise in the Irish town she'd called home for the last two years. Walking through the concrete streets where she'd chosen to live over there didn't appeal very much to either one of them at seven in the morning. Here, 7 AM took on a new life.

Pippa inhaled the cool sea air, relishing the refreshing saltiness. She hadn't realised how much she'd actually missed living on the coast until now. Spotting a piece of driftwood, she stooped down and snatched it out of a bed of seaweed, then watched as a small crab it was concealing scurried to find a new hiding place further in the bobbled green tangle of algae.

'Ginger. Fetch.' She threw the driftwood and Ginger raced off after it, quickly flanked by a black Labrador which hurtled past Pippa's legs, almost knocking her flying. 'What the—'

She looked over her shoulder for the owner of the dog and saw Oliver jogging towards her. That's when she realised the black Labrador was Jess. Oliver's eyes flicked from Pippa to their pets, but they were a little wide, showing Pippa he was a little worried about the welcome Ginger might give his pet. Pippa followed his gaze, and she too found herself a little nervous in case Ginger was suddenly spooked by this new dog coming from nowhere to go after his stick. She'd never socialised him with new dogs that way before.

Before Jess reached Ginger, Oliver whistled his pet and called her name. 'Jess. Come here, girl.' To Pippa's relief, Jess did as she was told and came bounding towards them, her tongue hanging out of the side of her mouth, which Pippa swore was part of her zany smile. Oliver grabbed her collar and swiftly attached the lead to it before patting her back. 'Good girl.' He straightened with a grimace. 'Sorry about that. I was running to join you with Jess at my side, but then you threw that driftwood and she went after it, too. It's her favourite thing to do on the beach.'

Pippa shook her head. 'No, it's fine. You have excellent recall with Jess.' She looked back over her shoulder and saw Ginger trotting triumphantly towards them with the driftwood between his jaws and his tail wagging. She quickly attached his lead to his collar and took the driftwood from him, stroking his head before tucking it under her arm. 'Good boy. Here's a new friend, Ginger.'

She watched closely as the dogs eyed each other, touching noses to sniff one another before their tails started wagging as they circled each other, sniffing more of each other.

Oliver's face broke into a smile. 'I knew it. They are destined for each other.'

Pippa's eyebrows shot up as Oliver looked up from the dogs to her face. 'Well, I'm not sure about that, but there is certainly a budding friendship building.'

'Is there?' The look in his eyes along with his question gave Pippa a strong reason to suspect he wasn't just referring to their pets.

She licked her lips. His penetrating stare was making her mouth dry and her palms wet. She nodded enthusiastically as she pointed to the dogs, wanting Oliver's intense glare to be anywhere but on her. 'Just look at them. It's adorable. I think we should walk awhile with them on their leads and then let them off. What do you say?'

'Perfect. Shall we head for the cove?'

Pippa gasped. 'I love the cove. It's my favourite part of this beach.'

Oliver's grin took up his entire face. 'Me too. I really missed it when I was in America. I have such fond memories of it. Catching miniature crabs there as a child, then smooching with you in my teens.'

Pippa could feel the weight of his stare on her profile, as if he was waiting for her reply, but she purposely chose to keep quiet about *that*. She'd thought of nothing else since she'd been on the beach that morning, but what good was talking about something that would never happen again?

They walked side by side in silence, watching their pets frolic with each other. It was Oliver who broke it. 'So, how has life been treating you since we last saw each other?'

Pippa turned her head to look at Oliver with a frown. 'Well, not that much has happened. I took a shower and went to bed.'

Oliver sunk his face into his hand and chuckled. 'Sorry. No. I meant since we last saw each other before I went to live in America. We've barely had a chance to speak, let alone catch up on each other's lives.'

His American drawl was on form this morning and it made Pippa's heart flutter. 'Oh right. Well, as you might have guessed by my profession, I studied marketing at university. Then when I graduated, I took a year out to travel around Europe with a friend from my student dorm. After that, I landed a position in a prominent firm where I stayed for six years, before deciding to go it alone. I started my own small business and became self-employed.'

Oliver glanced keenly her way as she spoke, nodding. 'And, erm, boyfriends?'

Pippa scoffed. 'Not much chance of that when one is trying to conquer a man's world at work by having to apply more effort to get the same acknowledgment as my male counterparts.'

Oliver blew out from expanded cheeks. 'I didn't realise sexism was still so prominent in this day and age.'

'How could you? You are a man.'

Oliver stopped walking and bowed. 'Let me extend my apologies on behalf of all my fellow misogynistic male counterparts.'

Pippa giggled. 'I accept the apology.' Oliver straightened with a grin. 'Besides, all that needing to constantly prove myself made me better at what I do. What about you?'

Oliver pointed down at their pets. 'Shall we chance letting them off before I regale my life's story?'

Pippa nodded. 'Yes, sure.'

They unclipped their pet's leads and watched in astonishment as they ran off side by side along the edge of the surf. When Pippa turned back from watching the dogs to look at Oliver, she was surprised to see he'd been studying her again and not their pets as she had been.

'My parent's divorce was a shock. It came from nowhere. As far as I knew, they were happily married. In fact, it was a shock to both sets of grandparents too, as it was the first divorce in both families' histories.' Pippa's mouth dropped open. 'It was tough. Especially when I was suddenly uprooted and made to live halfway around the world, away from my mother, grandparents and friends.'

Pippa's hand flew to her open mouth. 'I'm so sorry that happened to you.'

Oliver shook his head. 'It was okay in the end. I soon found my feet. It's either sink or swim in America. Only the fittest survive. I focused on my academic work and did my best in college, graduating with honours. Then, like you, I challenged myself to become the best in my working environment and chosen career. I set up my own company, and it's been growing ever since.'

Pippa nibbled on her bottom lip, suddenly shy to ask what was on the tip of her tongue. 'And relationships? Did you ever marry?'

She watched closely at how Oliver's eyes looked to the side, as if remembering a particular woman. 'There was someone...but it didn't work out. We were too similar.'

Pippa's stomach clenched and her chest tightened on hearing her childhood sweetheart had loved someone other than her.

The dogs barked in the distance, drawing both of their attentions. They were being petted by someone. Pippa glanced at Oliver. 'We'd better save that poor soul from getting slobbered to death.'

Oliver laughed. 'You still make me smile, Pippa Pickles.'

Pippa pointed a stern finger at Oliver, which didn't match the smile curling up the edges of her lips. 'Hey, what did I tell you about calling me that? Ollie *Onions*.'

'Why you—'

Oliver's body language showed her he was about to reach for her and tickle her, the way he used to back in high school when they were dating. She screamed an excited yelp and ran towards the dogs with Oliver close at her heels.

When she got closer to the figure, she could see it was Reverend Townsend. He was now down on his haunches, stroking both dogs, giving them a hand each. He looked up at Pippa and Oliver as they jogged towards him.

'Good morning. What a wonderful greeting I've just received from these beautiful puppies.'

Pippa raised her hand in greeting. 'Good morning Reverend. I'm sorry if they jumped up on you. They've only just met each other for the first time and they're a little excitable.'

The Reverend shook his head, dismissing her apology. 'No, they didn't. They were very well behaved. I love puppies so much. I really miss my Trixie.'

'I'm sorry to hear of your loss, Reverend. What breed of dog did you have?' asked Oliver.

The Reverend chuckled. 'Oh, it wasn't a recent loss. Trixie left me twelve years ago. She was a Jack Russell, but they are like family aren't they? Pets leave a whopping big hole in your heart when they are gone. It's so lovely to meet new puppies, though.' He looked at Pippa. 'I didn't know Brett had gotten a dog.'

Pippa shook her head with a smile. 'No, it's not dad's dog. Ginger is mine.'

The Reverend ruffled Ginger's fur. 'Ah, a perfect name for you, puppy.' He ruffled Jess's fur and looked up at Oliver. 'And what is this little puppy named young man?'

Oliver pointed to his own chest. 'I'm Oliver Oney Reverend.'

'Onions,' Pippa said under her breath so that only Oliver could hear. Oliver nudged her in the ribs and she stifled a giggle.

The Reverend's face lit up. 'Oliver. I didn't recognise you with your own facial fur.' They all laughed. The Reverend stood up straight and pointed down at Jess. 'What is your little girl called Oliver?'

'Jess.'

The Reverend stroked Jess's head. 'You are a pretty little thing.' He turned his attention back to Pippa and Oliver. 'I haven't seen you two in the village for a long time. Are you dating?'

Both of them quickly stole a look at each other before shaking their heads. 'No-no. We're both working in the pub for a few weeks, helping out,' said Pippa.

'Ah, right. Pity, we could do with a lovely wedding to look forward to.' Pippa's eyebrows shot up and Oliver beamed at her. 'I've been trying to boost the community spirits for a while now, doing this and that. The last thing we did as a community was months ago. I organised a best dressed property competition. The residents seemed to enjoy that, but I've not had a chance to do anything else since then.'

Pippa tilted her head as she remembered the uplifting effect the bunting had had on her when she drove into town. 'Is that why there is knitted bunting strung up on the beachfront handrail and on the houses there?' The Reverend nodded with glee. 'They were the first thing I noticed when I drove in. They are beautiful'

'Ah, I'm glad. We really need something else to raise spirits. Things just haven't been the same since lockdown.'

Oliver nodded. 'I know, I agree.'

The Reverend gestured towards the dogs. 'What about a local puppy competition? The pups could be scored on looks, obedience, and skills.'

Pippa looked at Oliver at the same time as he turned to look at her. 'We could hold it at the pub,' he suggested.

'Yes, and we could offer free doggy dinners to anyone dining there before or after the competition, beamed Pippa.'

'Yes.'

Reverend Townsend looked from Pippa to Oliver with a smile. 'Are you sure you two aren't dating? You seem to be very much in sync with each other.' Pippa's cheeks heated. 'This is fantastic. I knew there was a reason the Almighty sent me on an early morning walk along the beach today. If you get a poster done, I'll pop it up on the vicarage door and mention it in the weekend sermon.'

Oliver nodded. 'Great. I'll design one today, Reverend.'

'The Reverend nodded. 'Righto. I'm off to Katherine's cafe while I get a chance.' He shook his head. 'It's a shame Katherine won't be there for the summer season. I'll really miss those sausage twists.'

Pippa's mouth dropped open. 'What? But the café has only been open for a couple of years.'

'Katherine doesn't want to close. She's actually looking for someone to rent the shop from her. Come September, she has family obligations that might take her away for a few months.' The Reverend looked from one to the other. 'Do you know anyone who might be interested? Katherine has asked me to keep my ear to the ground. She doesn't really want to advertise it until she knows more of her family's circumstances.'

Oliver shook his head. 'Sorry, I don't.'

Pippa shook her head, too. 'Not that I can think of, but if someone comes to mind, I'll be sure to let you know.'

'Wonderful. Right. Time to put an end to my stomach growls. Any louder and they will be scaring the pups.'

Oliver and Pippa laughed. Pippa waved him off as he walked away. 'I'll drop the poster in when it's ready, Reverend.'

The Reverend held up his hand in acknowledgment without looking back as he headed back towards the road. 'You know where to find me.'

Pippa and Oliver turned to look at each other again. 'So, Pippa. Are you up for this doggy competition? If we get this right, this could be the first of many dog related community activities. We can do this.'

'We?'

Oliver shuffled his feet awkwardly. 'I mean your family's business can do this.'

Pippa smiled. 'It can only make things better. We are after all advertised as a very dog friendly pub and hotel.' Pippa checked the time on her phone. 'I need to get back. It won't be long before it's round two of the lunch-time meals.'

'Yup, me too. I have to drop Jess home, grab a shower and some breakfast, and then I have a cellar and bar area to prep.' They both laughed and called for their dogs as they ran playing chase across the sand with each other.

***

Pippa actually enjoyed the lunch time shift. It wasn't as busy as the day before, but there was a steady flow of customers. Oliver even helped out by being the server, taking the food from the kitchen out to customers when it was ready. Pippa enjoyed those brief snatches of time together the most. In between chatting about the dog competition and the doggy menu they could create, she could have sworn Oliver's banter while they interacted was verging on flirtation.

She almost protested when her aunt came to take over, asking if Pippa minded sorting out the clean towels for the new guests in the hotel rooms. It was nice to see that her father had also come down for the last half an hour to help in the bar.

At the end of the day, when all four of them were catching up on the day's events whilst sitting side by side at the bar, Pippa and Oliver told Brett and Morgan about the meeting on the beach with Reverend Townsend.

Morgan clapped her hands together in delight. 'Oh, that is a wonderful idea, isn't it, Brett?'

Brett chuckled. 'It really is. Why haven't we thought of doing it before now?'

'So you're okay if Oliver and I organise everything, Dad?'

Brett nodded. 'Yes, of course. I'll just serve the pints on the night and watch from behind the bar.'

'And I'll help out whoever is prepping and cooking in the kitchen. That reminds me, we need to place an ad for a new chef.'

'I'll sort it out, Aunt.'

'Thanks, Kiddo.' Morgan turned to look at Oliver. 'Does this mean you'll be judging the show?'

Oliver shrugged, 'Unless Pippa judges it. I'll probably be needed behind the bar.'

Pippa screwed up her face. 'Ugh, I don't think I could choose. I'd want them all to win. Maybe we should ask the Reverend.'

Morgan nodded. 'Good thinking. It was his idea, after all.'

'That's sorted. I'll ask him when I take the poster to the vicarage,' said Pippa.

Morgan turned to look at Pippa, giving her a special look. 'While we are all catching up, I need to let you both know, Brett and I will be going on that visit I mentioned to you Pippa, this weekend.'

Pippa's mouth opened when she realised the code behind her aunt's statement. 'No worries, Aunt. I'm sure Oliver and I can survive without you both.'

Oliver leaned on to the bar so he could get a better view of Pippa. 'Yes, Pippa and I make a terrific team.'

Pippa also realised there was more to Oliver's statement, and warmth spread in her chest.

Chapter seven

It was Friday morning. Pippa couldn't believe how quickly her first week back home had passed by.

That morning, Pippa's aunt had driven her father to a memory clinic after her aunt had made her aware earlier in the week a place had unexpectedly become available. With just Oliver and Pippa to cater for the lunch time needs of a very busy pub, it had been another exhausting day. Pippa barely had time to acknowledge Oliver when he'd come into the kitchen to pass on the food orders, let alone interact with him as they had every previous lunch time that week.

Once Pippa had cleaned the kitchen down and checked she had everything she needed for the evening meals, she couldn't wait to get back upstairs for a rest before it started all over again. She was looking forward to grabbing forty winks curled up on the sofa with Ginger, just as they often did in her apartment back in Ireland.

She left the kitchen and walked past the bar with her hand held up in a stationary wave, as Oliver was emptying the glass washer.

'See you later, Oliver. I'm going to have a cup of tea and a nap before we commence with round two.'

Oliver quickly placed the glasses he was holding onto the shelf and held up his hands in a stop gesture. 'Pippa, wait! Have you forgotten you said we'd update the pub's website today and plan some marketing strategies together to surprise your dad and aunt before they got back from their buying trip?' Her aunt had mentioned a visit in front of Oliver in the week, but

Pippa had elaborated later on, telling him they'd actually gone to a tradesperson's kitchen equipment event. She hated lying, but if her dad didn't want his own daughter to know about his dementia, he certainly wouldn't want anyone else knowing about it either. 'And didn't you say you were going to do an ad for more staff, too?'

Pippa slapped her hand to her forehead. 'Oh my goodness. Of course I did, that's right. We have to do it now in case we don't get a chance tomorrow.' She nodded her head. 'Okay, come upstairs when you've finished with your final jobs. I'll put the kettle on.'

***

Ginger was wagging his tail furiously when Pippa walked into the lounge. 'Hello my beautiful boy. Did you miss me?'

After fussing over him, she filled the kettle and switched it on, then she put Ginger's lead on him and took him outside to do his doggy toileting duties. When she made her way back upstairs to the living quarters above the pub, she found Oliver in the kitchen pouring the tea.

He looked back over his shoulder at her. 'Sugar?'

'Yes, Honey?'

Oliver's brow rose at her word of endearment.

Pippa crinkled her nose up and laughed at her own joke. She shook her head. 'Sorry, I couldn't help myself, I'm just getting you back for the jokey banter about eating ginger cake and biscuits. No...no sugar, thank you.'

Oliver's grin stretched from ear to ear. 'Are you trying to imply you're sweet enough?' He winked, joining in with the banter.

Pippa flicked her tongue around the perimeter of her lips, as if tasting herself. 'Erm, I think so.'

Oliver watched her tongue keenly, which made a delightful tingle dance the length of Pippa's spine. He looked as though he was considering kissing her.

Oliver all but whispered. 'I'd like to find out.'

Pippa was shocked. Had she heard him correctly? 'What did you just say?'

Oliver smiled, 'I said, this tea has some clout... Erm, is it Yorkshire tea?'

Pippa frowned. Was she hearing things she wanted to hear because she was still carrying a torch for Oliver?

She nodded. 'Oh...yes it is. Dad will only drink Yorkshire tea. He likes it because it's strong.'

Ginger bounded into the kitchen with his favourite cuddly toy in his mouth and headed straight for Oliver. Oliver went down on his haunches and ruffled Ginger's fur. 'I'd love to play with you buddy, but mummy and daddy have work to do.' Pippa's mouth dropped open. Daddy? What the heck did he mean by that? 'Mummy has to do techy stuff with me and daddy has gone with Morgan to shop for new kitchen equipment.' He glanced at her with a twinkle in his eye.

Pippa's hand lifted to her mouth. *Ohhh*. Oliver was referring to her father and the little white lie she'd had to tell him in order to conceal where her father had really gone this weekend. The realisation that he hadn't been referring to himself as daddy actually left her a little deflated. She liked the thought of Oliver being Ginger's daddy. That would mean she'd also be mommy to his fur baby—Jess.

Oliver's voice broke through her daydream. 'Shall I carry the tea through to the dining room? We can work on our laptops far easier in there side by side.'

Pippa blinked away her hazy daydream and nodded with a smile. 'Yes, perfect. I'll get my laptop.'

When she came back into the dining room, Oliver was sitting back in his chair at the dining table with Ginger balancing on his thighs as he tickled him behind the ears, and by the looks of both Ginger and Oliver's drooping eyelids, not much would be getting done anytime soon.

Pippa walked up to the table and placed her laptop down. 'You are a very naughty boy.'

Oliver's eyes opened wider. 'Oh, leave him alone. He's enjoying this.'

'I'm not talking to the dog.'

Oliver's brow shot up. 'What have *I* done?'

'You made me feel guilty for wanting to take a nap and there you are, practically face-planting your keyboard.'

Oliver shook his head, as if trying to wake himself up. 'Sorry Pippa. I've never felt so physically drained. I don't know how your father and aunt continue to work here at their age. Both sides of the business, the pub and the hotel, are physically exhausting.'

Pippa saw a chance to hint at them selling up. 'Nor me, neither of them are getting any younger. I wouldn't be surprised if they sold up and retired soon.'

'Really?' Oliver's interest appeared to be more than friendly concern. 'Although, it will be weird not seeing Brett behind the bar. When you think of The Cheese Wedge and Pickles, you think of Brett...and of course your lovely mother, Marie.'

The mere mention of the name Marie conjured up images of her mother laughing behind the bar and it made a lump magically appear from nowhere in her throat and tears brim on her lashes.

Ginger must have picked up on her change of emotions because he lifted his head and whimpered before jumping off Oliver's lap to paw at her leg. Oliver surprised her by jumping to his feet too and rushing towards her. He pulled her to him and encompassed her in his big, strong arms. 'I'm sorry, Pippa. I didn't mean to upset you by mentioning your mum. In fact, I've been wanting to offer my condolences since I met you, but there's never seemed an appropriate time. I-I really liked your mom.'

Pippa's nose was being pushed against Oliver's shirt and she couldn't help but inhale his personal odour. He smelt of day old cologne, musky soap and...him. Just how she remembered he used to smell way back in high school. But how was that possible? How could she remember *his* smell? It had been almost a decade and a half since she last laid her cheek on his chest.

Pippa sniffed back a sob. 'Thank you, Oliver. I'm not normally a weeping wreck. I think being back here again without her...amongst other things, has just got to me today.'

He grabbed hold of her shoulders and held her at arm's length to study her face. She immediately missed the closeness of him, then scolded herself for admitting such a thing to herself, even if it was just in her head.

She couldn't meet Oliver's eyes. If she did, she couldn't guarantee she wouldn't properly break down this time. 'Shall we make a start? Even if dad decides to sell the business, he still needs to update his website and hire more staff,' she said.

'Yes. If you're sure you are up to it.'

Pippa pulled herself from Oliver's grip. 'Yes, I'm fine. Honestly.' She sat down and pulled her laptop towards herself, opening it up.

Oliver walked around her chair and settled back into his seat. She could feel his gaze studying her profile. 'Just like old times, eh?' Pippa turned to look at him with a slightly puzzled frown. 'Studying in the library together after school,' he reminded her.

His comment made Pippa smile. 'Studying? Since when has stealing a quick kiss ever been classed as studying?'

Oliver's eyes twinkled. 'You remembered... Oh, to be young and carefree again, eh?'

The sadness Pippa felt a moment ago was now gone. They had been quite the young, loved up couple back in high school. It just wasn't meant to be. She could see that now, but at least they could be good friends.

Pippa shook her head. 'Yes to being young, but the pimples and the mood swings...no thank you. I like this age. I have my own place, a great job and a loving pet. What more could I want?' Oliver fell silent and his eyes roamed her face. Pippa squirmed under their scrutiny. If she was so happy, why did she have a nagging voice in the back of her mind keep repeating, 'he's the one who got away.' Pippa's hands flew to her face and onto her cheeks. 'What are you staring at? Have some of those pimples come back to haunt me?'

Oliver shook his head. 'No. I was just wondering. There was no mention of romance or a partner in that statement. Does that mean you're not interested?'

Pippa shrugged. 'I don't think I have any spare time to give to anyone.' She gestured towards her laptop. 'I mean, take now for example. This is supposed to be my, or should I say *our* free time and yet here we are, working.'

'Or not,' Oliver smiled.

Pippa shook her head with a grin. 'No, we aren't working, we're skiving. Come on, let's do this. If we get this all finished today with time to spare for a shower before we start the evening shift, I'll treat you and Jess to breakfast at Katherine's café in the morning, followed by a walk on the beach.'

'Deal.' Oliver held his hand out to shake on it.

They spent the next two hours absorbed in their tasks. Each one giving input on what the other was doing. By the time they'd finished, they had a new modern and updated website. Ads placed for the food side of the pub. Plans for future events they could hold in the pub that were guaranteed to draw in more custom, and an ad for a chef sent out to recruitment companies and posted wherever they thought they could attract one.

Oliver closed his laptop. 'Okay, that's me done. I'll see you later. Shall we say about 8'o'clock tomorrow morning for breakfast, too?' He winked in triumph.

Pippa nodded. 'On the dot.' She rose from her seat as well. 'I'll see you to the door.'

As soon as she closed it behind her, she checked her phone. There was a missed call from her aunt. She hit call back.

'Sorry I missed your call, aunt. I was doing some work and I left my phone on silent.'

'No worries, my darling. I was just calling to update you.'

'Yes, how's it going? Does he like it there? You know how fussy he can be with accommodation.'

'He likes the room, and he's actually doing really well with the memory tasks.'

'Oh, that is a relief.'

'How did the lunch time shift go? Was it busy?' asked Morgan.

'My goodness was it ever? After we closed, Oliver and I worked together to improve the website and do some marketing to drive new custom. Not that you need much more at the moment. I've never known it so at busy at this time of the year. I've made an advertisement to hire a temporary chef with the view to the position becoming permanent, as well.'

Pippa could hear the confusion and exasperation in her aunt's voice. 'I don't understand why you would do that Pippa, when I'm trying to persuade your father to retire and sell up.'

'I thought that's what you alluded to in the week when you said you'd work alongside whoever in the kitchen when it was the dog show.'

'Did I? Oh I'm sorry, Kiddo. I don't know if I'm coming or going lately.'

'You are also run off your feet at the moment seeing to dad's care needs. If you are serious about selling up, isn't it better to sell a flourishing business than a sinking ship? If I'm not here for any reason, it won't be easy for you on your own to keep up with this demand and oversee the food side of things, in addition to the hotel and my dad.'

Her aunt giggled. 'You remind me so much of your mother. She was always the brains, whilst your father was the entertainer. Of course, we need a chef. What was I thinking? Sorry for interfering Pippa, and I know you're not going to be here forever, so I'm grateful for everything you are doing right now.'

'Don't you dare apologise or thank me, Aunt. We are family and *you* have been dealing with a lot. It's *me* who should be apologising to you for my absence these past couple of years, thinking I could run away and create my own little impenetrable bubble where I could forget about all the memories from here and try to work through my grief isolated. It was very selfish of me to leave you and dad and abandon ship.'

'Hey, don't beat yourself up, Kiddo. We all deal with grief in our own way. Besides, the business is your mother's and father's. They didn't expect help from either you or your brother. You have your own lives to live, and anyway, I've always been here to help. We used to joke we were the three musketeers.'

'Thanks Aunt, you always have a way of making me feel better. Don't worry about anything. Oliver and I have things under control.'

'Oliver and you, eh? Hearing you say that takes me back.' Morgan chuckled.

Pippa laughed too. 'I thought you didn't remember about Oliver and my past relationship? You didn't appear to when I mentioned him...I'm ending this call now, before you remind me of how besotted I *used* to be about him. See you on Monday.'

Morgan laughed. 'Bye, Kiddo.'

Pippa ended the call and looked at her phone, shaking her head with a grin.

Chapter eight

Pippa sat at a table in Katherine's cafe, sipping coffee, waiting for Oliver and Jess while Ginger tucked into his breakfast at her feet.

When the door opened, she looked up to see Jess pushing her nose in through the gap of the door first, followed by Oliver. Her stomach did a little flutter. He looked unusually fresh-faced and handsome for such an early hour.

His face beamed when he spotted Pippa and a very excited Jess tugged him towards her and Ginger.

'Morning Pippa.' He looked down at Ginger who had finished his breakfast and was now sniffing Jess while she licked his empty bowl. 'Good thinking, feeding Ginger first. You never know how dogs are going to be with each other, eating together for the first time when they are both hungry.'

Pippa hadn't even given it a thought, but she took the praise with a smile and a nod, not wanting to feel foolish by admitting to the truth. Ginger had just been impatient after the first whiff of food. He hadn't stopped mithering her until his breakfast was in front of him.

'Morning Oliver,' called out Katherine over the music playing on the radio. 'I'll come and take yours and Pippa's orders in a moment.'

Oliver nodded as he took off his coat and slung it over the back of his chair. 'Thanks Katherine.' He pulled off his woolly hat and ruffled his hair before sitting down opposite Pippa. His dark waves fell naturally into perfection and Pippa couldn't help but think he was wasted working as a website designer. He would much better be suited adorning glossy men's magazines. No strike that—he'd be better adorning the cover of a Mills and Boon romance novel.

Pippa shook her head, ridding herself of the thought. Why was she thinking such things, anyway? This relationship was a working relationship built on an old friendship—period.

'Morning Pippa. Sleep well?' asked Oliver with a grin.

Pippa nodded. 'Morning. Yes, like a log. To be honest, I could quite easily have skipped breakfast for a couple of extra hours in bed.' She shuffled in her seat under his intense stare. Did she still have sleep in the corners of her eyes or something? She discreetly checked. No. Then why was he studying her face as if she was the *Mona Lisa*?

His lips peeled back into a smile. 'We've already had thirty views on the website since I published the new updated version last night, which according to the analytics is an increase of sixty-five percent compared to the normal daily quota.'

Pippa's smile matched his. 'Wow. That's amazing.'

Katherine approached the table with a pen and notepad poised. 'Are you ready to order?'

Oliver gestured towards Pippa. 'Ladies first.'

Pippa smiled and turned to look up at Katherine. 'A small English breakfast for me please, with scrambled eggs and a glass of orange juice please, Katherine.'

Katherine scribbled the order down and looked up from her notepad at Oliver. He clapped his hands together and rubbed them with glee. 'I'll have a large full English breakfast please with fried eggs, a cup of tea and a glass of orange juice.' Jess whimpered by his side. 'Oh, I almost forgot Jess. Can I order a doggy breakfast too?'

Katherine went down on her haunches and tickled under Jess' chin.' Did your naughty master almost forget about his little girl?' Ginger pushed under Katherine's arm not wanting to be left out. She laughed and ruffled the fur on his head. 'Yes, I know you are a good boy for eating all of your breakfast.' She picked up Ginger's empty bowl. 'Ten minutes, guys. I'll make your drinks, then I'll prepare your food.'

Oliver nodded his head. 'Thank you, Katherine.' He turned back to Pippa. 'So, any news?'

'About what?'

'Kitchen units and appliances.'

'What?' For a moment, Pippa hadn't a clue what Oliver was talking about. Then she remembered the white lie she'd told him about her father and aunt's whereabouts. 'Ohhh. No. They haven't seen anything in their price range.' She shrugged. 'I suppose it's just as well, considering they might sell up.'

Oliver nodded in agreement. The café door opened, drawing both of their attentions. A woman dressed for the artic pulling a huge suitcase behind her entered. Her mouth dropped open when she saw Oliver.

'Oliver? I wasn't expecting to see you in here.'

'Ava? I-I can't believe you are here...What-what exactly are you doing here?'

'I came in here to ask for directions.'

Pippa looked from the beautiful blonde woman with an American twang to Oliver. He shook his head. 'No, I mean what are you doing in England?'`

'Oh. I came to England to meet with potential clients. I knew you lived here somewhere by Seagull Bay, so I booked in The Cheese Wedge and Pickles Hotel and thought I'd kill two birds with one stone, meet my clients and try to track you down. How luckily am I finding you in here?' Ava looked at Pippa, as if just registering Oliver was not alone. She walked over to Pippa, offering her hand. 'Hi, I'm Ava. Ava Garland. A very close friend of Olivers. And you are?'

'Erm, Pippa. Pippa Pickles, erm I mean *Bramwell*...Pippa Bramwell.'

Ava giggled. 'For real? Are you sure about that?'

Pippa frowned. 'Yes.' She looked across at Oliver for support, but his face looked as if it was watching an approaching bus with no brakes. 'I'd offer you a seat, but my dog isn't too welcoming with strangers.'

Ava looked down at the dogs. 'Really? Neither of these little bow wows looks vicious to me. In fact, that white one looks as if it might lick me to death.'

'Gold,' Pippa corrected.

Katherine appeared with a tray of drinks. 'Oh hello, I didn't realise I had another customer.'

Without giving Ava a chance to answer, Pippa lifted her mobile. 'I'll call through to The Cheese Wedge and Pickles for you and let them know you are on your way. My family owns it, so I can make sure there's someone to meet you at the entrance.'

She stood up and handed Ginger's lead to Oliver before heading for the door. Oliver took it open-mouthed. She looked back over her shoulder before she left and saw Oliver pointing in the direction of the hotel.

Pippa crossed her fingers and hoped Lizzy, the woman who helped out with housekeeping would answer the phone. Her chest felt tight and her body was jittery. Was Ava an old girlfriend from Oliver's time living in America?

Thankfully, Lizzy answered immediately.

'The Cheese Wedge and Pickles hotel. How can I help you?'

'Oh, thank you for answering, Lizzy. There's an American woman called Ava Garland who is booked in for a stay. I'm in the café and she came in asking for directions. Do you mind awfully opening up early, meeting her at the door, and signing her in?'

'Not at all, Pippa. I suspect she's going into room five, as I've just finished cleaning it.'

'Yes Lizzy. Thank you. I'll be back in an hour.'

'No problem, Pippa.'

Pippa inhaled deeply and turned to go back into the cafe. She stepped back inside and was relieved to see Ava hadn't taken a seat. She walked over to the table and caught the end of Oliver's sentence. '—three o'clock on Tuesday then.'

'Perfect,' said Ava.

Pippa coughed and Ava spun around to face her, sparkling white teeth still bared from her smile at Oliver. 'All sorted. Lizzy is waiting to show you up to your room. The hotel is just across the beachfront. You probably didn't see it when your taxi dropped you here because the view of the sign for the hotel is obscured by a tree from here.'

'Thank you.' Ava turned back to Oliver. 'See you Tuesday, Oliver.'

Oliver smiled and nodded. Ava pulled her suitcase towards the door and Oliver jumped to his feet, handing both Jess' and Ginger's dog leashes to Pippa so that he could run in front of Ava. 'Here. Let me get the door for you.'

'Thanks Ollie.'

Pippa fumed inside. *Ollie. That's my nickname for him.*

She sat down at the table and Oliver sat down opposite her just as Katherine arrived with their food, helping to diffuse the air of awkwardness that had now appeared between them.

'There you go. One small breakfast. One large one...and one doggy meal.' She looked from one to the other. 'Can I get you anything else?'

Pippa pushed out a smile. 'No thank you, Katherine. This looks wonderful.'

Oliver picked up his cutlery wrapped in a serviette. 'And smells amazing. No, thank you.'

Katherine laughed lightly. 'Enjoy.'

Oliver placed Jess's food on the floor and both Pippa and he glanced at each other before eating. They ate in silence for a minute or two, but Pippa couldn't hold in her curiosity any longer. 'So...your close friend came for a surprise visit?'

Oliver chewed for a few seconds nodding and swallowed before answering. 'Yes. It's a real surprise because I haven't seen Ava in years.'

'Or spoken to her?' Pippa raised her brows, curiosity brimming inside her after remembering Oliver saying last week he needed to make a call to America.

Oliver had taken another bite of food again. He held his finger up, requesting a moment to finish eating. Pippa swore she could see cogs turning behind his eyes.

'It's been a while.'

'How did you meet?' She was never usually this nosey, so why was she acting like the Gestapo now? Oliver's personal business was just that—personal. It had nothing to do with her.

COMING HOME TO SEAGULL BAY 89

Before he could answer, Pippa's phone rang. She picked it up from the table and studied the screen. She didn't recognise the number.

'Hello?'

'Hi, I'm calling about the job advertised in Chef's Weekly.'

Pippa couldn't keep the surprise from out of her voice. 'Really? The job's already on the site?'

'Erm, yes. It is still available isn't it?'

'Yes-yes, it is. Sorry, what's your name?'

'Declan. Declan Riley.'

'Right Declan. Sorry, let's start again. Hello, I'm Pippa. You've caught me at a slightly awkward moment. Can I call you back in thirty minutes?'

'Yes, of course.'

'Can I call you on this number?'

Oliver watched her closely, the same curiosity she had for Ava burning in his eyes.

'Yes.'

'Okay great. Speak soon.' She ended the call and looked across the table at Oliver. 'A prospective chef.'

Oliver smiled. 'Wow. That's great. At least we know the job is appealing if you're already getting enquiries.'

Katherine re-appeared. 'Everything okay?'

Pippa nodded. 'Mmm, yes. This is lovely.'

Oliver agreed. 'Fantastic.'

'Good. Any more drinks?'

Oliver shook his head. 'Not for me. We're taking the dogs to the beach soon.'

Pippa shook her head, too. 'Just the bill please, Katherine.'

'I'll get this,' Oliver said quickly.

Pippa shook her head vehemently. 'No way. It was my suggestion.'

He held his hands up in a surrender position. 'Okay, but I'll get the next one.'

Pippa lifted her eyebrows. 'So we're doing this again?'

'Breakfast and a walk on the beach with our pets? I'd like to while you are here. Wouldn't you?'

'I guess I would...that is, if you have time to fit me in.'

Pippa wanted to poke herself in the ribs for the snidey comment. It was so unlike her. Thankfully, Oliver didn't reply. He just studied her briefly. His silent judgment made her want to shrink in her own skin. She turned her back on him and made her way to the counter to pay, sucking in a long breath in her brief respite.

Katherine smiled warmly at Pippa as she handed her a twenty-pound note. 'Thank you. What are your plans for the day, Pippa?'

'A walk on the beach, maybe a little light reading, and then the first shift of the day. Thank you, that was divine, Katherine.' Pippa could see Oliver putting his coat on in her peripheral vision.

Oliver lifted his hand. 'Yes, superb Katherine. Thank you.'

Katherine rung up the till and handed Pippa her change. 'I'm glad you enjoyed it. Have a great day you two. I'll see you later. I plan on having my evening meal at the pub tonight.'

'Great, see you later. Katherine.'

Oliver was holding the door open for Pippa as she approached it. She turned her head to look at him as she stepped through the door. 'Thank you. You are somewhat of the gentleman today, aren't you?' She silently scolded herself under her breath. 'Stop that Pippa.'

His double-edged comeback made her smart. 'I just can't help it when I'm in the presence of such beautiful *women*.'

Not only was he complimenting her, he was complementing Ava, too. It served her right.

Pippa instantly shed her jealousy and pulled her mouth into a pleasant smile. 'Shall we head for the cove?'

'Sure.'

Ten minutes later, Jess and Ginger were running up and down the beach together and frolicking like a pair of love struck teenagers.

Watching them lifted Pippa's spirits immensely. She analysed her earlier behaviour as they walked silently side-by-side on the wet sand and surmised she was subconsciously worrying about her father and selling the pub. Who would buy it if he agreed to sell? It had been her family home and business her whole life, plus it played an integral role in the community.

If it were sold to the wrong person and made into a commercial monstrosity, it could have a serious detrimental effect on their small town life, something both Oliver and Pippa had recently agreed needed invigorating.

'Penny for them?' asked Oliver.

Pippa drew her attention away from the dogs and turned to look at Oliver. 'What?'

'You have been miles away for the last ten minutes.'

She pursed her lips and squeezed out a small smile. 'Oh, I was just pondering on the future of the pub if dad were to sell it. The buyer would need to have the community's best intentions at heart. But there's no guaranteeing that, is there?'

Oliver didn't answer, but looked thoughtful. 'I must admit Pippa, since you told me last night about the possibility of the pub and hotel going on the market, I've thought of nothing else.' He stopped walking and turned to face her. 'I'd be very interested in buying it myself. The only problem is, I'm not sure I'd be able to afford it. I'd probably need to seek the help of a sleeping partner, but then that brings its own issues. Such as, would the partner be as sentimental about the business as I would be because it's more likely than not that he *or she* wouldn't be a resident of the village?'

Pippa's mouth dropped open. Oliver was the last person she would have expected to show interest. He already had a successful website building business. He wouldn't have time to commit to both.

'But what about your business?'

Oliver shrugged. 'I'd be willing to sell it. That's how strongly I feel about this.' Pippa closed her mouth and looked towards the dogs as she processed the revelation. 'I can't read what you are thinking about from your features, Pippa. What are your thoughts about it?'

Pippa was stunned he cared what she thought. They hadn't seen or heard hide nor hair from each other in years, and it wasn't as if they weren't working closely together through choice. She turned back to him with a smile. 'I think you would be the perfect fit for the place.' Oliver sighed a huge sigh of relief and his shoulders visibly dropped a few inches. 'I'm so relieved to hear that. Shall we head back? We can talk more about it later.'

Oliver's soft brown eyes held her gaze and her tummy fluttered. 'Yes, I'd like that.'

Pippa hastily pulled her phone from her pocket. 'Shoot. What's the time? I need to call the applicant back about the job.'

Chapter nine

Pippa didn't get the hour of peaceful reading she hoped for. She'd forgotten she'd booked an early morning appointment to get her hair trimmed, washed, and blow-dried. She hastily made her way to the little hairdresser shop that had been the first place she'd ever gotten her hair cut by a professional.

She smiled to herself as she remembered the fringe her mother had tried unsuccessfully to give her with a pair of kitchen scissors after telling Pippa she had always dreamed of being a famous stylist for the stars.

Pippa had willingly sat there in their kitchen as her mother promised to make her look like *Baby Spice* from the *Spice Girls*, a pop band she'd adored growing up. A small chuckle escaped her lips as she remembered the ragged edge of the freshly cut fringe her mother had given her, making her hair look more like the edging bricks of a turret, and not the slick and sharp edge she'd hoped for.

She'd bawled her eyes out. Oh, how she remembered the look of devastation on her mother's face at her own mess-up. Thankfully Christine, the only hairdresser in the small town-village, had been able to immediately fit her in with an appointment to rectify her mother's good-intentioned mistake.

Her grin from the memory was still tugging up the corners of her mouth as she walked into the hairdressers, tinkling the same bell above the door that had notified Christine of her arrival all those years earlier.

Christine came out from the back with a beaming smile. 'Pippa. It's so lovely to see you again. How long has it been since you were last in here?'

'Too long, Christine. Look at the state of me. I've found a lovely little hairdressers close to my home in Ireland, but it's been closed for a few weeks due to a bereavement. They are good, but they are not a patch on you, Chrissy.'

Christine laughed and patted a seat by the washbasin. 'Bless you. Hang your coat up and come and sit here. I'll wash it first and put the kettle on, and then you can explain to me what you want doing this time.'

Pippa laughed. 'What do you mean this time?'

'You always seem to be sporting a new hairstyle each time I see you.'

Pippa grinned. 'I suppose I do.'

'I'm not complaining. I wished more people were like you. It would keep me constantly busy instead of the sporadic days I'm seeing lately. Some days I'm busy from opening to closing time. Other days, I barely have enough customers to pay for the electricity I use.'

Pippa felt sad for Christine. 'Have you ever thought of a side-line business venture? Dog grooming maybe?'

Christine laughed. 'That is actually a really good idea, Pippa. I'm not laughing at the idea of it, more at the thought of me doing the grooming. I wouldn't have a clue. I'm more of a cat person. I've never owned a dog in my life. Not that I don't like dogs, I just love kitties more. There is a room at the back I could use, which at the moment is just a storeroom. Maybe I could convert it.'

'Or you could hire it out.' Pippa suggested as she settled in front of the washbasin, holding her arms out in front of her for Christine to slip a gown on, before draping a towel around her shoulders, too.

Christine looked thoughtful. 'You might be onto something there, Pippa. There are lots of families living around here with dogs. They must go into one of the bigger towns to get their pooches groomed. You know, Tom will be here shortly to fix a leak. I'll ask him to take a look at the storeroom to see if it's a big job to get plumbed.'

Pippa grinned widely and winked at Christine as she lay back with her head over the washbasin. 'I'm not just a pretty face you know.'

Christine turned on the water and checked the temperature before she held it over Pippa's hair. 'I know. That's why you started your own business and moved to Ireland.'

Pippa felt a stab of guilt. The move to Ireland had nothing to do with her business a she'd alluded to when she'd first told people of her move. She couldn't exactly tell them she was moving away because she wasn't coping with her grief at being in the place she felt was haunted by her mother's absence.

'I'm actually here for a while now, Christine.'

Christine's eyebrows rose, her interest piqued. 'Really? Not just a fleeting visit this time?'

'These days, I can work anywhere as long as I have my laptop and internet, so I thought I'd spend a month or so here. I've missed this place. Funny really. When I was a kid, I dreamed of living in a vibrant city anywhere in the world but here,. But now I'd take this quiet little coastal town over the noise and toxic fumes of city life all day long.'

Christine worked up a lather in Pippa's hair. 'They always come back—the young folk. Take young Oliver Oney for example. He was gone for years. Now he's back. Looking devilishly handsome too, and with an accent that would charm a woman before he'd even finished his sentence.' Christine sighed and giggled. 'If only I were thirty years younger.' Pippa giggled too as she looked up into Christine's pale blue eyes. 'Didn't you two date back in high school?' she asked.

'Geez, your memory is phenomenal, Christine.'

Christine laughed. 'I get to hear it all in here. I always say that other than one's mother, the hairdresser is the best person to confide in. Plus, I listen closely to the chatter of others when they sit and have a chat whilst getting their hair done.'

Pippa whistled. 'I bet you've heard some juicy tidbits of gossip over the years.' Christine nodded as she washed the suds away before applying conditioner. 'Yup, but my lips are sealed. Hearing gossip is one thing. Spreading it is another.'

'I hear that,' said Pippa.

The door tinkled, announcing the entrance of another customer. 'Good morning Tom. I'll be with you in a second. I just need to finish washing my client's hair.'

'Morning Christine... Is that Pippa Bramwell I can see?'

Pippa's mouth stretched wide on hearing Tom's voice. 'It is. How are you, you old rascal? I haven't seen you in the pub since I've been back.'

Tom's voice was melancholy. It immediately caught Pippa's attention. 'I've been away. I've just come back from holiday. It was supposed to be the start of the next chapter in my life...but it's not the chapter I thought it would be.'

Christine gasped. 'Are you okay, Tom? Is Jenny okay? Nothing bad happened to her on the cruise did it?' Christine washed the remaining conditioner from Pippa's hair and began to towel dry it.

'No, nothing like that... She-she finished things between us. Our relationship ended on the cruise.'

Christine wrapped the towel around Pippa's head and rushed over to Tom to embrace him. 'Oh, I am sorry, Tom. I never saw that coming. She seemed perfect for you. I've never seen you looking so happy.'

Tom huffed. 'Six months we were together. I'm never using one of those darn dating apps ever again.'

Christine rubbed the side of his arm. 'Crikey. I was going to register and try one myself after seeing how happy you were, but I don't think I'll bother now.'

Tom placed his hands on her shoulders and furrowed his brow as he stared down at her. 'Please don't let my misfortune put you off, Christine. You might find the love of your life.'

'He's right Christine. Just because it hasn't worked out for Tom, doesn't mean the same thing will happen for you.' Pippa smiled through thin lips at Tom. 'Sorry to hear that, Tom.'

Tom shrugged. 'Just not meant to be, I suppose.'

Christine smiled up at Tom and glanced back over her shoulder at Pippa. 'Sorry love, I've abandoned you. Come and sit here in front of the mirror. I'll show Tom where my leak is and I'll put the kettle on now.'

Christine ushered Tom through a door and Pippa sat in the chair she had indicated. She thought about how well suited Christine and Tom were. Maybe if the dog show went well, she'd also suggest hosting a dating night at the pub. Maybe she could get her aunt hooked up with someone as well. It had been years since her aunt had been in a relationship. She filed the idea away in the back of her mind.

Pippa looked at herself in the mirror. A little water had splashed in her eyes and she'd rubbed them. Now she looked like a panda. She grimaced at her reflection and pulled out a pack of wipes from her handbag. Thank goodness she'd thought to pack them. With her wet, bedraggled hair and panda eyes, Pippa thought what a sorry state she looked.

The tinkle from the bell above the door drew her attention, and she sucked in a shocked breath when she saw Oliver's American friend standing in the doorway—glowing, with not one strand of hair out of place.

Ava pulled her perfect brow together as she studied Pippa. 'Oh sorry. I didn't recognise you. I'm looking for the stylist.'

Pippa rubbed at the black kohl below her bottom lashes. 'Erm, a blob of shampoo got into my eyes,' she offered freely as a way of explaining her appalling appearance. Another little white lie. She hoped God would understand—circumstances and all. Ava smiled in acknowledgment. 'Christine will be out soon. She's with the plumber,' she quickly added. They smiled at each other, and the awkward silence between them drew out as the seconds ticked by. 'Is everything okay with your room?'

Ava nodded. 'Yes. It's very quaint. My girlfriends couldn't believe how small it was when I skyped them. One even joked her closet was bigger.' Pippa fumed inside. 'I told her it reminded me of the bedroom inside the mini wooden palace my father built me in my backyard when I was a kid. I think the hotel room is the most adorable place I'd ever slept in.'

Thankfully, Christine came out before Pippa's tongue could run away with her and tell Ava the words she'd rather keep inside her head.

'Hello, can I help you?'

'Hello yes. Could you fit me in for a wash and style?'

'Oh, you have almost the same accent as Oliver.'

'Oliver Oney?'

Christine smiled and nodded. 'Yes. Do you know him?'

'Yes, that's who I'm getting my hair styled for. We have a date.'

'Oh, how lovely. Going anywhere special?'

'Into the city later on today.'

Pippa's brow drew together, forming a deep rut. 'Erm sorry to butt in, but I thought Oliver was working in the pub today.'

Ava shrugged. 'Oh, I don't know anything about that. All I know is, Oliver is collecting me at one PM.' She dismissed Pippa and turned back to Christine. 'So, could you fit me in say, an hour?'

Christine nodded. 'Perfect. I'll have finished with my other client by then.'

Ava smiled and headed for the door. 'Fantastic. See you then.'

She left, leaving just the smell of her strong perfume behind in her absence. Christine picked up a comb and a pair of scissors and stood behind Pippa. 'What a surprise. Do you think that's Oliver's girlfriend?'

'I-I don't know. Excuse me a moment, Christine, while I make a quick phone call.' Pippa took her phone from out of her bag.

'No problem, Pippa. I'll pour the tea and check on Tom.'

Pippa was grateful Christine still used a teapot to make her tea. She dialled her aunt Morgan's number.

'Hello aunt. Is Oliver not working today?'

'No, not the day shift. He's got some business meeting to take care of. Your father and I will help out today instead. He'll be there for the evening shift, though. Why have you seen him?'

'No. Just the woman he's having his *business* meeting with.'

Morgan laughed. 'Do I detect a hint of jealousy in your voice?'

'No, not at all. I just wanted to make sure you knew about him so that the shift was covered...we've been busier than normal lately. In fact, I'm interviewing someone later this evening for the part-time chef position.'

'It's fine. It's all sorted. Where are you?'

'Getting my hair trimmed, then I'm going to get supplies. Anything you want fetching back?'

'No, thank you. Got to go. Your father is calling me.'

'Okay aunt. See you later.'

Christine emerged from the back room with a cup and saucer in each hand. 'I'm not sure whether you take sugar, so I've left two sugar cubes on your saucer.'

'Thank you.' Pippa took the saucer and placed it on the dresser below the mirror.

Christine combed Pippa's hair back. 'A trim and blow dry, isn't it?' She looked at Pippa's eyes through the reflection. 'And I'm guessing you're going to call in later too, to buy a can of hairspray to keep your style in place.'

Pippa frowned. 'Huh?'

'After the mysterious young American woman's appointment.'

Pippa's eyebrows rose. 'Ahhh. Yesss. I need to go to the farm shop and old Ben's first, but by the time I've finished, my hair will *definitely* need holding in place.'

Christine winked at Pippa and Tom appeared.

'Fixed. It was just a faulty washer.'

'Oh wonderful. How much do I owe you, Tom?'

Tom shook his head. 'Nothing. Maybe a trim?'

Christine beamed. 'If you don't mind little ol' me instead of a barber, I'll gladly cut your hair for you anytime. How about this afternoon? Any time after three. I want a little advice about a project I might be planning for my storeroom.'

Tom nodded as he walked towards the door. 'That's a date.'

He exited the shop, and Pippa winked at Christine. 'I might be calling in here tomorrow morning as well for another can of hairspray.'

Christine belly laughed. 'You cheeky beggar.'

***

After getting the supplies, Pippa parked outside Christine Cuts hair salon, and fluffed out her hair as she walked towards the door, making a fuss about the volume of it in case anyone who was looking that way earlier had seen her go in, and now was watching her mysteriously return. She didn't want to draw suspicion. There was nothing worse than hearing gossip about herself in her own pub.

Christine was sitting in one of the client's chair sipping a cup of tea and looking out of the large glass shop window as Pippa entered. 'Get everything you needed?'

'And some more. There's no predicting how busy we will be at the moment. Monday, Tuesday and Wednesdays used to be our quiet days, but they are just like weekend days at the moment.'

'Don't knock it. I wished they'd call here for a quick trim first.'

Pippa made a sympathetic face. 'I heard you ask Tom to come back later to take a look at your storeroom. I'm glad you are considering dog grooming. We are after all, a very friendly dog community.'

Christine nodded. 'Yes, it makes sense. Thank you for the idea... Now, have you come back for that tin of hairspray?' Christine added a wink.

Pippa fluffed out her hair again. 'Oh, you know I have.'

Christine patted the other client seat next to hers and Pippa sat down. 'Well, here's what the American lady *freely* told me. Ava used to date Oliver five years ago.' Pippa's mouth dropped open. 'He designed her website. That's how they first met. Her work is her priority, and they never got to see much of each other, so their relationship sort of fizzled out before it even had a chance to get going. She's here for work and as Oliver still does updates for her website, she said she thought she could kill two birds with one stone on her visit here.'

'So she's here to see Oliver in a working capacity only?'

Christine took a sip of her tea. '*That*...I cannot answer. I can only relay what she freely told me. Although she appeared to be very excited about the lunch date she was about to embark on.'

Christine studied Pippa closely. 'You're still carrying a torch for him, aren't you?'

Pippa's eyebrows almost disappeared into her hairline. 'No! Not at all. I'm just as curious as you about the American stranger, that's all.'

Pippa's phone rang, and she quickly fished it out of her pocket. She checked the caller ID. It was her aunt. 'Hello?'

'Hello Pippa. Are you getting the fish order while you are out?'

'Yes aunt, I've already been and got the fish and other supplies from the farm shop.'

'Thank goodness. I just received an advanced booking for a large group coming to visit the town in a minibus.'

Pippa's eyes widened as she looked up at Christine's wall clock. 'I'm on my way.'

Chapter ten

Pippa and Morgan sat at the bar and sighed simultaneously as Brett closed the pub doors. He leaned back against them and groaned. 'Ugh, we could have done with Oliver here. My hips are killing me now. I had three barrels run out one after the other. I didn't think I was going to make it back up from the cellar after I'd re-connected the third one.'

'You head on up, Brett. Pippa and I will sort out the bar and cash-up ready for this evening's shift.'

Brett shook his head. 'No. I'm not leaving all the jobs for you girls. It's not fair. You've already worked hard enough in the kitchen.'

Morgan pointed her finger towards the door, which lead out to the stairs and up to the living quarters above the pub. 'Go on. That's an order.'

Pippa nodded in agreement. 'Yes, go up, Dad. You'll be good for nothing if your arthritis flares up any worse than what it already is now.'

Brett nodded and rubbed at one of his hips. 'Thanks girls. I think I will go up—if I can make those darn steps, that is.'

Pippa and Morgan watched Brett disappear through the door, and then Pippa blew out a long breath. 'I agree with Dad. We really could have done with Oliver today.'

'Oh well. We survived didn't we? And Oliver won't be here for much longer, so we'll have to get used to working without him. At least until we sell the pub.'

Pippa stared at her aunt's face, trying to read it for signs she was hinting the pub was going on the open market soon, but Morgan had a good poker face. 'What are you suggesting, Aunt?'

'Your father finally agreed with me. We're getting someone in for a valuation tomorrow.'

Pippa's eyes widened, and her mouth dropped open. 'Really?' Morgan nodded. 'I can't quite believe it's happening.'

'Are you upset, Kiddo?'

Pippa gauged the sudden tightness in her chest and ball in her stomach and nodded. 'Yes, I think I am. The thought of strangers living here is...*weird*.'

Morgan rubbed her hand up and down the small of Pippa's back. 'I know, but with neither you nor your brother interested in taking over the business, your father has no other option. Plus, he's nearing retiring age now, anyway. A few years earlier than planned won't hurt—especially considering the circumstances.'

Pippa grimaced as she was reminded of her father's dementia, which she had carefully filed away in the back of her mind once he'd returned from the memory clinic. Her face pulled tight, and she turned to face her aunt. 'Guess who told me he was interested in making an offer if he could get a sleeping partner?'

Morgan's brow creased into a row of lines as she raised it questioningly. 'Who?'

'Oliver.'

'What?! When?'

Pippa looked sheepish. 'Sorry, I might have accidentally mentioned the pub might be going on sale to him.'

Morgan's mouth dropped open. 'Oliver? I thought he was happy and doing well with his own business?'

Pippa shrugged. 'All I can tell you is he expressed a genuine desire to own the pub. Apparently, he's wanted to work here since he was old enough to, but never got the chance because of his move to America.'

'Hmm. That's interesting. I wonder who the sleeping partner would be.'

'Possibly an American.'

'What?'

'That's where he was today, meeting an American for a business date.'

Morgan scrunched up her nose. 'I'm not sure about that. What if this American wanted to make the pub all commercialised?'

'Unfortunately, you wouldn't get a say in it. Once you sign the contract and hand over the key, the new owners can do whatever they want with the place.'

Morgan's face fell. 'Oh well. As much as it would pain me, whatever is best for your father is my only concern—I made a promise to your mother that I'd look after him and I'm not about to break it. If it wasn't for your parents taking me in and giving me a job after Bren's sudden passing all those decades ago, I don't know what I would have done. They were different times back then. You didn't get as much help from the government as you do today.' She placed her hand over Pippa's and squeezed. 'Come on. Let's finish up before we drop. We can discuss Oliver's *possible* interest if he decides to put in an offer when the pub goes up for sale. Until then, let's not worry ourselves about it.'

***

Pippa was already in the kitchen making the preparations for the evening meals when Oliver popped his head around the door. 'Morgan tells me you were all rushed off your feet at lunchtime.'

Pippa looked up from what she was doing and tried to keep the annoyance from her face. 'Yes, it knocked my dad about. His arthritis still hasn't settled down... Good meeting was it?'

The furrow in Oliver's brow ironed out, turning his face expressionless as he nodded. 'Yes. Definitely worth the effort. I just wished it could have been held in the hours the pub was closed.' Pippa remained silent and looked back down at what she was doing. There was no point causing bad blood about it. Oliver was after all, helping out her family. He didn't have to be there, but they'd be stuck if he wasn't. 'Erm, I'd better get back to it.' She nodded without looking up.

The evening was just as busy as the lunchtime opening hours had been. Morgan went from bar to kitchen, helping out. Pippa had completely forgotten about the prospective chef coming for an interview until Morgan came into the kitchen and put her apron back on. 'He's here. Next to the pool table.'

Pippa looked across at the exhausted face of her aunt. 'Who's here?'

'Declan Riley. The chef who's come in for the interview.'

Pippa's hands flew to her face, instantly covering her cheeks in flour. 'Blimey. I'd forgotten all about him.' She peeled off her apron and flew through the door.

'Pippa! You've got—.' But she had already disappeared before Morgan could finish her sentence. 'Oh, never mind.'

The pub was bursting at the seams, but it didn't stop Pippa from instantly spotting Ava perched on a stool at the end of the bar—close to Oliver.

Pippa felt her blood heat. She looked immaculate. Her perfect white teeth gleamed underneath her open-mouthed, full smile. The pillar-box red lipstick on her full lips was bleed free. And her blonde hair was still set in the long bouncy waves Christine must have teased it into earlier in the day.

Oliver looked at Pippa with a frown as she passed by the bar. Pippa felt her stomach drop into her feet at his obvious disgust at her appearance compared to Ava's. Was he secretly judging one against the other? Pippa gave him daggers and marched towards the pool table, forcing herself to smile at locals who waved and greeted her as she passed them by.

'Hello Pippa, no Brett this evening?'

'Great steak pie, Pippa.'

'Are you here long?'

'How you finding Ireland, Pippa?'

Pippa didn't answer the many questions, she just held her hand up with splayed fingers, indicating she needed five minutes.

Declan was sitting at a small table to the left of the pool table. He rose to his feet as she approached him with a warm smile spread across a handsome, close-shaven face. Pippa held out her hand and Declan grabbed it and shook it firmly. 'Declan, thanks for coming. Did it take you long to get here?'

Declan shook his head. He had hair as dark as night cut short into a crew cut. 'No, less than half an hour. The short distance from where I'm living at the moment to here is one of the factors that made me apply for the position.'

Pippa glanced back at the bar before she sat down and she could see Oliver craning his neck to see who she was talking to.

She spent the next thirty minutes getting to know Declan and laughed freely at his jokes. He reminded her of her brother. Every time she glanced over at the bar, she caught Oliver looking her way. From his interview, Declan was proving to be a very good fit for the pub. He was in between jobs due to a failed relationship in which he'd shared a business and living accommodation with his girlfriend. That meant he was living short-term at a friend's house and looking for somewhere more permanent to live. He told Pippa he would be looking for a property to rent closer to the small town if he got the position. The commitment instantly sold him to her.

'Could you start tomorrow?'

Declan's face lit up. 'Yes. What time shall I come in?'

'Erm, ten thirty?'

'I'd like to come in a little earlier for the first few days, if you don't mind, so that I can get familiar with the appliances. Cookers all tend to have their own cooking times, nothing like their settings.'

Pippa laughed. 'It took me three days to realise that.' She stood up, and Declan followed suit. 'See you in the morning.'

Her smile was as wide as her face as she spun around. She headed for the bar, excited to inform Oliver, but slowed when she remembered Ava was still in the same seat, just feet away from him.

Oliver looked from Pippa to Declan as he walked behind her to exit the pub, before returning his gaze back to Pippa while trying to keep his cool. 'New boyfriend?'

Pippa's eyebrows rose as she shook her head. 'No. Declan will be our new part-time chef.' She was amazed to see his shoulders lower as he relaxed on hearing her answer.

The feminine American drawl joining in with their personal conversation made Pippa's teeth clench. To her annoyance, Ava had been ear-wigging. 'Good job he's not your man. He was probably cringing with embarrassment when those snow-white cheeks come towards him in this crowded bar.'

Pippa looked past Oliver to the mirrors behind the tiered bottles of alcohol and gasped when she saw her reflection. She looked like a ghost. Her face was almost completely covered in flour. She forced out a smile and pointed to herself. 'What this? This was part of a test I set for the new prospective chef, and he passed with flying colours.'

'Oh, what test was that?' asked Oliver.

Pippa's mind scrambled, trying to think of an answer. She could see Ava twisting in her seat, equally curious. She glanced at Ava, drawing attention to her unwanted involvement in the conversation. 'I'll tell you later. I need to get back to the kitchen to help Aunt Morgan.' She turned on her heels and sped towards the kitchen door humiliated. The only useful thing the flour had done all night was to cover her burning red cheeks as she escaped her embarrassing episode.

Back in the kitchen Pippa let out a long sigh. Morgan looked back over her shoulder at her from the pile of pans she was washing up. 'How did it go?'

'Declan is perfect. I offered him the job, and he's starting tomorrow.'

Morgan's face split into a smile, which faltered. 'Then why the huge sigh?'

'You could have warned me, aunt. I looked a right fool in front of the physically perfect American woman sitting at the end of the bar when she pointed out I looked like an extra from *the Michael Jackson Thriller video*.'

'She said that?' Her aunt's voice hitched in disbelief.

Pippa shook her head. 'Not those exact words, but I was mortified all the same.'

Her aunt sighed. 'I *did* try to warn you, but you didn't hear me. You ran out of here like a bull at a gate.' Morgan placed the last pan on the drainer and picked up a towel to wipe her hands as she turned fully to face Pippa. 'Is she still here? The American?'

'Go have a look. With that tan and glowing smile, she stands out like a sore thumb against the pasty locals in here.'

Morgan chuckled. 'Now-now, sarcasm is very unbecoming and doesn't suit your caring nature. Anyway, since when have you ever bothered with what people think of you?'

Pippa forced a smile. 'I don't.' She shook her head, as if trying to shed the skin of the woman she was a moment ago. 'She just makes me feel…inferior.'

'You are both very beautiful women, but your beauty is natural and classical. You are an English rose and you are in full bloom right now. You are stunning my dear. I don't think you realise how many admiring glances you get.'

'Really?'

'Really. Especially from a certain bearded bar tender.' Pippa's mouth dropped open. 'Talking of Oliver, when we close tonight, should we tell him about the estate agent's visit tomorrow?'

Pippa quickly recovered from her aunt's astonishing statement. She didn't want to let on how much it had affected her. 'Let's wait until we hear what the valuation is first. I wanted to go over what we are doing in the dog competition tonight because the event is in two days and I'll be pre-occupied showing Declan what's what tomorrow.'

'Okay, Kiddo. Right, that's the washing up done. If you don't mind, I'm going to turn in for the night. I'm exhausted.'

Pippa walked over to her aunt and wrapped her arms around her, squeezing her in a loving hug. 'Thanks aunt. At least it will be a little easier in the next few months here with Declan on board now.'

'You are a treasure, Pippa. If I'd have been blessed with a daughter, I would have wanted her to be just like you.'

Pippa welled up. Life had been cruel to her aunt. First, the love of her life was taken from her in a tragic accident after just a couple of years of marriage, then according to the doctor, shock had made her body succumb to ailments they couldn't diagnose until a decade later. She'd been a fighter though, not letting the days when her health was at its worst stop her from working at the pub with Pippa's parents. Secretly, she was Pippa's hero.

Staying in the kitchen and giving it a deep clean ready for Declan's start the next day, Pippa didn't even know the customers had left and Oliver was about to lock up until he poked his head around the door.

'You'll wear yourself out.' Pippa jumped with a start. He grinned. 'Sorry, didn't mean to startle you. You do realise you are the last man standing—or should I say woman? I'm about to close up for the night.'

Pippa's face blanched. She'd been so engrossed in getting the kitchen perfect, she hadn't even realised it was silent in the pub. 'Has everyone left?'

'All except us... I was expecting you to come back out to the bar and tell me all about the new chef.' Oliver pointed to her hair and opened the door fully ready to walk towards her. 'You've got a stray—'

Pippa swiped the stray strand of hair away before Oliver took it upon himself to come and move it for her. She didn't think she could handle the proximity tonight—not after her aunt's comment. 'I got it.' She crossed her arms and held his gaze. 'You appeared to be a little *preoccupied* this evening, so I thought I'd leave you be, even though we need to work out a plan for the dog competition.'

Oliver shuffled uncomfortably from foot to foot. 'Oh, you mean with Ava? Well, after our business meeting, I felt obliged to offer her a drink in the pub being as I was rushing off from the meeting to start my shift here.'

'Boy. That sure was a long *business* meeting.'

Oliver narrowed his eyes. 'How do you know how long it was?'

Pippa licked her lips and subconsciously patted her hair. 'Oh, I just happened to be at the hairdressers when Ava popped in to book an appointment. She mentioned she needed it done by a certain time because of her...date.'

Oliver's face flushed, and he shoved his hands deep into his pockets as he shook his head. 'No, no. It wasn't a date per se. It was a catch up with a business oriented purpose.'

Pippa held her hands up. 'Hey, what you do in your spare time has nothing to do with me.' She turned her back on him, inadvertently dismissing him. Plus, she needed to hide any trace of jealousy her face might be betraying. 'Don't worry. I'll turn all the lights off. See you tomorrow.'

She picked up a cloth and began wiping the already pristine table. Her heart beating rapidly as she waited for Oliver to answer. But she was waiting a long time as there was a long drawn out silence instead. She turned to face him again and was surprised to see he'd walked a few steps towards her and was directly behind her. She'd never heard him.

Her eyes widened as she looked up into his deep brown eyes fringed with equally dark lashes she'd been envious of when they were teenagers. Her chest rose and dropped from her heavy breathing. Oliver's lips parted as he looked down at her mouth. The air tingled with tension. Was he going to kiss her?

His finger reached up and brushed over the tip of her nose. 'You missed a bit of flour.'

He turned his back on her and strode out of the kitchen, not even looking back as he said night. 'See you tomorrow, Pippa... Night.' He hadn't even wished her a *good* one.

Pippa's stomach turned over as she watched his large shoulders disappear through the door. His cologne wafted up her nose and added a flutter in her chest to go with her quickening heart rate. She sighed and forcibly threw the cloth into the sink. Why was he always having this effect on her? Oliver had been just a childhood sweetheart.

But he was the one who got away...said her inner voice.

'Shut up,' she said to herself as she turned the light off.

Act 3 - Chapter eleven

Pippa was just returning from her walk on the beach with Ginger when a motorbike passed her and pulled up in front of the pub. The man riding it had a tattered leather jacket on and faded blue jeans. He looked like he was shooting a commercial for 501 jeans. She watched mesmerised as the rider dismounted and unclipped the strap under his chin. Intrigued by who would have such a great body, Pippa waited with bated breath for the helmet to be removed so she could see who it was.

Declan turned to face her with an impish grin. 'Morning Pippa. Is it okay to leave my bike parked here?'

Pippa's grin reached from ear to ear. 'Declan. I wondered who the mysterious man was.' She nodded. 'Yes, it will be safe there. Wow! That bike is amazing. How long have you been riding a motorbike? I've always wanted to have a ride on the back of one.'

'Since I was sixteen. I'll bring a spare helmet one of theseedays and take you for a spin if you like?'

Pippa nodded eagerly. 'Yes please, that would be awesome.' She lifted her phone to check the time. 'You're early.'

'I hope you don't mind. I wanted to get my bearings around the kitchen and study the menu.'

Pippa shook her head. 'Not at all.'

Declan pointed to Ginger. 'Is he friendly? Can I stroke him?'

Pippa nodded, 'Yes and yes. If you don't mind being licked to death.'

Declan walked over to Ginger. Going down on his haunches, he placed his helmet on the ground beside him and ruffled Ginger's ears. 'You are a handsome boy.' Ginger lifted his front paws onto Declan's knees, almost sending him falling backward, and proceeded to give him a doggy wash.

A bark from behind made Pippa turn around. It was Oliver and Jess. Oliver looked at Declan frolicking with Ginger and then looked at Pippa, his chin jutting out as if he was disgruntled by what he saw. 'I was just about to call on you to see if you and Ginger fancied an early walk on the beach.'

'Oh, we've already been for a walk.' Declan stood up and Pippa gestured to him. 'You've met Declan haven't you?'

Oliver shook his head. 'No, it was Morgan who spoke to him last night.'

Declan smiled and held his hand out, stepping forward to shake hands with Oliver. 'Hi, you are the barman aren't you?'

Oliver eyed Declan's hand for a moment before he took it, shaking his head. 'No. I run my own website company. I'm just helping *close* friends out in a tight spot.'

'Ah, right. Hi. I'm Declan, the new chef.'

'Oliver—the close friend.'

Pippa watched on bemused at the introductions and the very firm handshake that followed. She turned to Declan. 'I'll let you in and show you to the kitchen.'

Declan released Oliver's hand and nodded. 'Great.' He picked up his helmet.

Pippa turned to Oliver. 'Why don't you ask Ava?' Oliver's brow lifted. She instantly regretted saying the words as soon as they'd tumbled from her lips.

'Ask Ava what?'

'To go for a walk.'

'Good idea.' Oliver turned his back on her and tried to walk away, but Jess was sniffing noses with Ginger, her tail wagging furiously, refusing to follow. 'Come, Jess. Ginger has already been for a walk.'

Pippa's stomach knotted as she looked at how happy their pets were together. Ginger would be upset if he didn't get to see Jess again. Oliver finally managed to pull Jess away and strode away purposely.

'Have a good walk,' Pippa called after him, but he either didn't hear her, or he chose to ignore her.

Pippa mustered a smile, even though her chest felt tight, and turned to face Declan. She gestured towards the door at the side of the pub. 'Shall we?'

***

The dinnertime shift ran smoothly. Pippa stayed in the kitchen with Declan, standing back on the sidelines and only interjecting when he appeared unsure of something. She was impressed. He was a true professional and he'd naturally fallen into the role as if he'd worked at the pub for years.

Pippa was baffled by Oliver's behaviour each time he brought a new food order through. He appeared to spend longer than usual in the kitchen with them than he'd done any time previously when Pippa had worked in there alone. It made her wonder if he was as jealous of her with Declan as she was of him with Ava.

When the lunchtime shift was over and Pippa and Declan were cleaning up, Oliver appeared again. 'I thought we'd better discuss the dog competition seeing as it's tomorrow. Are we planning on doing any special doggy related meals?'

Declan stopped what he was doing and turned to look at Oliver. 'A dog competition? Are employees' pets allowed to join in?'

Pippa spun to face him with a growing smile and wide eyes. 'Oo, I suppose so, but only if there is someone to represent them on their behalf. What breed of dog do you have, Declan?'

Declan grinned. 'A St Bernard. He's partly the reason why things didn't work out between my ex and me. She wasn't really a dog lover.'

She gasped. 'What? Who wouldn't love a St Bernard? Gosh. I bet he's huge. The friend you're staying with must be very patient.'

Declan shook his head. 'Not really. That's why I'm desperate to find somewhere else to live.'

Oliver stepped closer, almost cutting in between Pippa and Declan. Pippa frowned, but Declan didn't appear to notice. 'I saw an ad on the notice board in Katherine's cafe for a room to let. A room in a dog friendly house.'

Pippa smiled up at Oliver. She thought there might have been a touch of working rivalry between them, but she was wrong—and pleased.

'Really? Where is this café?'

'Just across the seafront square.'

'Thanks, I'll go and check it out as soon as I've finished work. As for dog inspired food, you could still serve part of the normal menu, but run a themed menu alongside it, like hotdogs and burgers named after breeds of dogs? I could make our own burgers and the meals could be served up to both owners and pets in dog bowls.'

Pippa clapped her hands together excitedly. 'I love that idea Declan, and I can get the ingredients from the farm shop.'

Oliver looked from Pippa to Declan, his features remaining stoic, his mouth set in a thin line. 'Sounds as though you've got this covered between you. I'll see you later, Pippa.'

Pippa's mouth dropped open as she watched Oliver storm out of the kitchen. She didn't want him to think she didn't need him, because she did. Her mind scrambled for something that would keep him in the thick of things. She shouted after him. 'Oliver, I need your help. Could you ask the Reverend to judge the competition? I forgot to ask him when I dropped off the poster!'

His face poked back through the door with a limp grin. 'Sure. I'll go now.'

Pippa spread a full smile across her lips. 'Thank you. See you later.' He nodded and disappeared. The tightness that had spread across Pippa's chest when he'd stormed out eased slightly.

'He seems like a really nice guy...*slightly intense*, but nice,' said Declan.

Pippa laughed lightly at Declan's comment. Oliver was far from intense—normally, but he had been acting a little odd around Declan. Maybe she was right about the rivalry. 'I think he has a lot on his mind at the moment.'

Pippa thought about her reply. She was defending Oliver's behaviour to Declan. Why?

He was the one who got away. Her inner voice answered her question.

'We're just friends.'

'Sorry?' asked Declan.

Pippa shook her head with a smile, realising she'd answered herself aloud again. 'Oh, I was just saying, Oliver and I are friends who go way back.'

Declan nodded his head slowly. 'Ahhh, that explains the big brother, protective attitude then.'

'What?'

Oliver continued to explain with an impish grin. 'I noticed it straight away. The way he didn't take his eyes off you when you were interviewing me. You had your back to the bar so you didn't see it. Then the way he acted around you this morning. And then, just now.'

'Just now?'

Declan looked up as if remembering something. 'Actually, he was acting more like a jealous lover than a big brother just then.'

Pippa crumpled her face into an incredulous scowl as she shook her head, but her face didn't reflect the thrumming of her excited heart at hearing Declan literally declare that he thought Oliver was jealous of her spending time with him. 'No. We are totally in the friendship lane.'

Declan winked. 'I hope you don't think I'm talking out of place as this is literally my first day on the job, but I think you need to be aware Oliver might be straying out of lane.'

Pippa's mouth dropped open and her heart beat quicker. 'What gives you that impression?'

'I'm a man. I can tell when another man finds a woman desirable.'

Pippa's cheeks exploded with colour. 'I-I need to go buy those dog bowls. Morgan will be down soon to let you out before she locks the side door. Thanks Declan. See you later.'

She stumbled from the kitchen, trying to avoid Declan's gaze to hide the weight of her embarrassment. She was embarrassed because Declan had got it wrong. It was more the other way round. She'd been the one continuously glancing back at Oliver during the interview. She'd been the one acting weird this morning and just then when Oliver had come into the kitchen. Oliver was just reacting to *her* weird behaviour when she was around him.

She shook her head. 'You'd better pull yourself together, Pippa.' She ran upstairs to the living quarters and the home she'd always known above the pub. Her father was asleep in his armchair soundly snoring with an open suduko book on his lap and his pencil still poised between his fingers. Her aunt was heading for the door as she walked in.

'How did things go with Declan? I was just coming down.'

'Fantastic. He's just finishing the preparations for tonight. I've come up to grab Ginger and take him with me to buy some dog bowls.' On hearing his name, Ginger leapt to his feet from his cosy spot between Brett's feet. He bounded over to Pippa, barking. 'Shhh, you'll wake dad.'

'Too late. I'm awake.'

'Sorry dad.'

'Where's Marie?'

Pippa's eyes widened, and she looked across to Morgan. Morgan smiled sweetly at Brett. 'You've just woken up. You're all disorientated. Did you have a dream about Marie, dear?'

Brett blinked his eyes and then stared straight ahead, as if comprehending where he was. He looked over at Pippa and Morgan and blinked again. 'Oh. Yes, I did. It was a wonderful dream. We were at the community bar-b-que. Marie looked so beautiful. She was standing next to Phil and Jenny, and Pharis was taking their photo.'

Pippa remembered the poster Pharis had given her. She hadn't told her father or Morgan about it in case it upset them, but this was the perfect opportunity to reveal it.

'I have something to show you both. Pharis gave it to me the other day.' Pippa rushed into her bedroom and quickly re-emerged with the cardboard cylinder. She prised the lid off and pulled out the poster. She placed the cylinder down and unravelled the poster, holding it up.

Brett gasped and Morgan did a little happy chuckle. 'That is exactly what I saw in my dream. Oh, I do miss her.'

Pippa heard him stifle a sob. Her stomach instantly contracted into a tight ball. She quickly passed the poster to Morgan and ran over to her father, flinging her arms around him. 'I really miss her too, dad, and if truth be told, that's why I moved out. It was just too painful being here without her. I'm so sorry I abandoned you.'

Brett patted his daughter. 'I know Pip. I knew that was the reason. You didn't abandon me. You were here for the first twelve months, but then you had to do what you thought best. I was perfectly happy with your decision to move out.' He chuckled. 'Heck, most kids move out as soon as they can.'

Pippa did a small laugh. 'I was spoilt. I had a wonderful family and I didn't want to leave.'

Brett laughed lightly. 'We are a good family aren't we? Your wonderful aunt, bless her, she's been my backbone ever since we lost your mom.'

Morgan swept his compliment away with a flick of her hand. 'Get off with you, Brett. You and Marie have been a shoulder for me to cry on plenty of times. Yes, you are right, we are a good family. We're here to help each other—through thick or thin. That's why you've never been able to get rid of me... Now, I'm off downstairs before my mascara grows legs.'

Pippa looked up to watch her aunt leave with a smile of affection spread across her face. She looked back down at her father and kissed the top of his head. 'She's right, dad. Just like Aunt Morgan, I'm here as long as you need me.'

Brett reached up and cupped Pippa's cheeks. 'Thank you, my darling girl.'

Ginger whimpered and barked. Pippa straightened. 'Okay boy. We're done with the mushy stuff. I know it upsets you. Come on. Let's get your lead on and go shopping.'

Brett chuckled.

***

Pippa felt as if a weight had been lifted from her shoulders as she walked to the local hardware store.

If old Po didn't sell dog bowls, then she'd have to drive out of their small town to one of the horrible retail parks with the huge pet stalls that were killing small businesses and communities by undercutting them, just because they could buy in bulk.

Pippa was amazed so many small businesses in their town still kept going. She supposed that was a credit to the community spirit she thought was dwindling. She kept her fingers crossed old Po had dog bowls. Po sold everything—he always had done.

On her very first trip to the shop with Brett, when she was just a small child, she'd been amazed by the twigs he'd sold in a pot on the counter. Po had given her one for free, stating it was healthier to chew on the stick than a sweetie. She'd remembered how odd she thought Po was, handing out twigs instead of sweets. That was until her father said it was okay to accept it and try as the twigs were natural roots. She couldn't believe it when the twig root had tasted exactly like liquorice.

Pippa walked into the shop and it was like going back in time. Not a thing had changed. Stainless steel pots were still strung from the ceiling in the centre of the room and stock was strategically placed alongside a natural walkway to the counter. As she made her way to it, she passed piles of welcome mats, stacks of buckets, bundles of broom sticks. You named it and it was sold at Old Po's. There was so much to see. It was as if she were in a museum for hardware. 'Hello?'

She heard dragging feet and then the small bent over frame of Po came shuffling out from a back room. He lifted his crooked neck and looked under the brim of his flat cap. 'Hello. Can I help you?'

Pippa's heart melted. Like Ben the fisherman, Po hadn't changed a bit—well apart from the fact that he looked two feet shorter, or was that because she had grown? She did a quick recall of the last time she'd been inside the shop and was astonished to remember it was in her early teens when her mother had sent her to fetch a new mop and bucket.

Pippa's smile spread across her face. 'I really hope you can. I'm after dog bowls.'

Po lifted his cap and scratched the top of his head in thought. 'Dog bowls, eh? I think I've still got some, although the young folk prefer to get fancy ones these days from those superstores. What they don't realise is, those big stores only care about the profit. They don't care about the customers so much.' Po shuffled slowly out from behind the counter and Pippa followed him as he made his way over to a corner of the shop. 'If my memory serves me correctly, they're here somewhere.'

He began to move cardboard boxes out of the way. Pippa hovered behind, towering above him, stepping from foot to foot, eager to help, but unsure if it would be accepted. 'Need any help to find them?' she finally resorted to asking.

'Goodness me. No. I wouldn't dream of letting a customer haul supplies about. It's all part of the service my dear.'

She sighed a silent breath of relief when he finally found them because he sounded to her like he was gasping for breath after the exertion. He handed one to her. 'Is that what you're looking for?'

Pippa smiled. 'Perfect, but I need more than one.'

Po lifted his bushy grey eyebrows and looked down at Ginger sitting by Pippa's feet. 'Eat a lot does he?'

Pippa shook her head. 'No, it's not for him. I need as many as you have for a theme night.'

Po frowned. 'You want dog bowls for a theme night?' He shook his head. 'You young ones do weird stuff these days. I can't watch half of what plays on the picture box anymore. It's all nonsense.' He reached for the stack of stainless steel bowls fit snuggly inside each other. 'This is going to work out expensive, flower.'

Pippa had to hold in her chuckle. Picture box? Was he referring to the TV? 'As long as I'm helping a local business and not one of those *superstores*, I don't care how much they are going to cost.'

Po tuned around to face her, holding onto the bowls tightly in his weathered old hands. His smile almost disappeared in an avalanche of wrinkles, but it showed off the brilliant white of his dentures perfectly. 'I like your way of thinking young girl. Follow me and I'll give you some discount.'

***

Pippa couldn't get the smile off her face as she walked across the beachfront square towards Katherine's café. Seeing old Po again really made her appreciate her small coastal town and the unique privately owned shops and businesses it had.

Small towns and villages with privately owned family-run businesses and thriving communities where everyone knew their neighbours and looked out for each other were becoming rarer to find. She made a silent promise to herself she'd do everything in her power to persuade whoever bought the pub to try to revive their community spirit again.

She was just making a mental note of what she would say to whoever brought the pub when Ava emerged from Katherine's café laughing. Pippa stopped in her tracks when she saw Oliver at her heels, laughing too, obviously sharing the same joke.

Pippa dived behind a tree, dragging Ginger with her.

Ava looked back over her shoulder at Oliver. 'I'll see you tomorrow at the Wedge pub.'

'Looking forward to it,' said Oliver.

Pippa almost dropped the bag of bowls. Who was she kidding—she almost threw the bowls down.

'Wedge pub! It's called The Cheese Wedge and Pickles you ignoramus.'

Chapter twelve

There was a light rap on Pippa's bedroom door. 'Pippa. There's a parcel that's just arrived for you.'

Pippa screwed her closed eyes even tighter, trying to think if she'd ordered anything online to be delivered at her dad's address before she'd left Ireland. 'Okay, thanks Aunt. I'll be out soon...can you put the kettle on '

Her aunt popped her head around the door. 'I've just made a fresh pot of tea.'

'Blimey. You're up early this morning.'

'More like you're getting up late, Kiddo. Check your clock. Don't worry, I've already taken Ginger out to do his business and fed him. Now I'm going downstairs to let Declan in.'

Pippa shot bolt upright when she saw that it was 10'o'clock. 'Oh my goodness. I meant to set my alarm. It's the dog competition today. I have a ton of stuff to do.'

'No you don't. Declan will prep the food. All you need to do is decorate the pub.'

Pippa sat still for a moment to gather her thoughts. Was that all that needed doing? Her mouth lifted at the corners. 'I think you're right, Aunt Morgan.'

Morgan smiled. 'Oh yes, there is one more thing I need to tell you. The estate agent will be here in thirty minutes.' Her head disappeared as she closed the door behind her before Pippa could reply.

Pippa was mid-stretch and yawn and the news made her immediately stop and jump out of bed. She quickly slipped her feet into her slippers as she tugged on her dressing gown. There would be no time to take a shower and wash her hair now. She looked in the mirror and groaned when a human cockerel stared back at her. She grabbed her brush and raked it through her hair, trying to detangle the unruly curls and get rid of the hump in her hair that lifted unnaturally high. It was no use. She'd have to wet it, and hope that would do the trick.

Brett was sitting at the kitchen table munching on a slice of toast. He looked up at her with a frown when she walked into the room. Ginger got up from by his feet and bounded over to her with a doggy smile and a very waggy tail.

Pippa rubbed his ears the way he liked her to do in the mornings. 'Are you happy to see me, boy? I bet you're excited for today, aren't you?'

'No school today, Pippa?'

Brett's comment stopped Pippa in her tracks and her breath caught in her throat as her mouth dropped open. 'School?'

Brett shook his head and screwed his eyes shut. 'Sorry my darling, I meant work. I know you don't go to school anymore.' Pippa exhaled the breath she'd sucked in. 'Is your car in the garage or something? Do you need a lift to Porters?'

Pippa's insides twisted into a knot. 'I-I don't work at Porters anymore dad, I haven't worked there for nearly eight years.'

Brett's brows drew together, forming a deep rut between them and his eyes were downcast as he looked from side to side as if trying to remember. He looked back up with the rut ironed out. 'Of course you don't. Oh don't get old Pip, it does funny things to you.' Her father winked and gave her one of his silly grins.

Pippa tried her best to return the grin, but inside, her world had just crumbled. This mistake was definitely not a slip of the tongue. Her appetite instantly disappeared. She walked over to her father and kissed the top of his head. 'I'm going to get dressed Dad. The estate agent will be here soon.'

'Oh yes... So, your Aunt Morgan told you about the plans to sell up and have an early retirement?'

'Yes, she did.'

Brett grimaced, as if unsure of Pippa's response. 'What do you think about it?'

'I think it's a wonderful idea. You've worked damn hard ever since I can remember, Dad. You deserve to slow down... Especially now your arthritis keeps flaring up.' Pippa hoped that would put his mind at ease.

His shoulders appeared to visibly drop, and he nodded quickly. 'Yes-yes, my arthritis...Morgan said the same thing.'

Pippa could see by the look in his eyes he was still conflicted by the idea. She placed a hand on his shoulder and squeezed. 'Then you shouldn't feel guilty about it, Dad. Lots of people retire early with ill health.'

'Do they? I've not heard of anyone in our community retiring early. I'm worried about what they might say.'

'They won't say anything, Dad. They know you have Oliver here to help out at the moment because your arthritis is giving you jip. I'm sure they'll understand. I think you've done your time.' She laughed lightly to try to lighten the atmosphere. 'If you'd have committed murder, you'd have done your time twice over by now.'

The joke brought the smile back to Brett's lips. 'I have missed you, Pip, and your daft jokes.'

Pippa smiled, feeling better now she'd made her dad see reason, and headed to the bathroom.

Twenty minutes later, she was washed, dressed and had applied a little make-up. She viewed her appearance in the reflection of the mirror. The hair flick was still sticking up, but she didn't have time to faf about with it anymore.

Her father was sitting in front of the TV watching the news. Ginger trotted back over to him and lay down in his usual spot between his feet. 'I'm going down Dad. See you later.'

He turned to look at her with a smile and pointed to the sideboard. 'Okay Pip. Don't forget about your parcel.'

Her chest lightened. *She had* forgotten about the parcel, but her dear old dad had remembered. Was she worrying needlessly about his mental health?

'Thanks Dad.'

She grabbed the parcel and headed downstairs to the pub, opening the box on the way down. Inside were two keyrings, a letter and instructions. She stopped to read the letter before opening the door leading into the pub lounge.

The keyrings were actually dog collar tags, and inside them trackers were fitted. The instructions were for the app that needed to be downloaded and set up to be able to use them. A new company had heard about the competition and had sent one of the keyring trackers as a prize, and the other as a gift for the organisers.

Pippa pushed open the door and walked into the pub with a smile. She was surprised to see Oliver was already there hanging the box filled with decorations for the competition.

He was up a set of stepladders hanging the last line of bone-shaped bunting.

'Morning Pippa, you look happy.'

Pippa held up the tracker tags to show him. 'Look! A new company has heard about our competition and they've sent us two dog trackers. One is to offer as the first prize and the other one is for us, the organisers.' She stretched a hand forward, offering one. Here, you had the idea about the best dressed dog event, so you have it.'

Oliver shook his head. 'No, I insist you have it. You've done most of the work for it.'

Pippa grinned. She was secretly pleased. Although Ginger was good at coming back when his name was called, the recall she had with him wasn't anywhere near as good as Oliver had over his pet, Jess. Pippa was always nervous, letting Ginger off his leash somewhere new. A guilty ball formed in her stomach. She knew she hadn't spent as much time on his training as she should have done getting him whilst still in a very low stage of grief.

'Thank you.' Pippa gestured to the doggy bone bunting. 'It appears you've already put up the decorations. I came down a little earlier to do them before going into the kitchen to see if Declan needs any help.'

Oliver put his hands on his hips and surveyed his handy work. 'Not bad, eh? I'm quite looking forward to it now.'

Pippa beamed, 'Me too...Oo, what time is Reverend Townsend coming?'

Oliver's face fell. 'I forgot to tell you, when I called in to ask him if he'd judge the competition, he informed me he was very flattered to be asked, but he'd have to decline. He needs to cover another parish's duties because its vicar was ill. He has a funeral to attend to today. He apologised profusely because he'd bated us with the idea, but said god would provide us with a replacement.'

Pippa gasped. 'But who? We needed a non-resident—someone impartial.'

Oliver grimaced. 'The only person I could think of on the spot was my friend Ava. She'll be here soon.'

Pippa tried her best to pull up the corners of her mouth, although she knew the smile she was conjuring wasn't reaching her eyes. 'Good thinking. She won't know who are local residents and who have entered the competition from outside the community.'

Oliver's shoulders dropped as he sighed. 'I'm so glad you approve.'

'Why wouldn't I?' said Pippa, drawing her brows together.

Oliver rubbed the back of his neck, appearing a little uncomfortable. 'I don't know…I'm sorry. I don't know what gave me that impression.'

Pippa shook her head. Her long wavy hair swished around her shoulders. 'She seems like a really lovely woman.' She gestured towards the kitchen. 'I'd better see if Declan needs any help. Time is ticking.'

Oliver nodded. 'Yes-yes, I need to check on the bar too.' He pointed down at the floor. 'See you here in thirty to go over everything with Ava?'

'Yes…see you in thirty.' Pippa couldn't walk away quick enough. She was seething, but she had no reason to. Ava was perfect for the job as a judge. She would be impartial.

She pushed open the kitchen door and was astonished to see Declan had already prepared everything.

He looked up from chopping something and smiled. 'Morning. I've had a great idea that will make things a lot easier if we're busy. I hope you don't mind, but I've changed the menu.'

Pippa's brow rose, almost meeting her hairline. 'What? I'll-I'll have to print out new menus.'

Declan's face crumpled. 'I forgot about that. Sorry. I just thought it would be so much easier if we had just one meal available for both dogs and their owners. Something that could be served to them both in dog bowls.' Pippa cocked head to the side seeing reason, even though her gut was tightening again as she worried about getting the new menus changed and printed off before things got busier upon the arrival of Ava. '*Paul Watters*, a chef whose column I follow in the New York Times has a smoked sausage casserole recipe that will be perfect.'

Pippa nodded calmly, trying not to show Declan the panic building up inside. 'Okay, if you think that will be better.'

Declan nodded eagerly with an enormous, toothy grin. 'Yes, I do. That's why I took the liberty of preparing to serve that instead.' He handed her the recipe.

'Right okay. If there's nothing for me to do in here, I'll go and change the menus.' Declan nodded and returned his attention to his chopping.

Pippa blew out from inflated cheeks as she opened the kitchen door and walked out into the pub lounge. Ava was already there, a hand resting on Oliver's shoulder and laughing with her head tilted back. Her blonde hair cascaded down her back in perfect curls, as if she was fresh out of the salon.

Oliver's face was beaming, and it was hard to miss his hand resting on Ava's hip. Had she interrupted an intimate moment? Her chest tightened.

Oliver looked in her direction, and his face registered surprise. His hand dropped quickly from Ava's hip. 'It's only been five minutes. Have you finished in the kitchen already?'

Ava turned to look at Pippa. Was that a smug smile? She made no attempt to drop her hand from Oliver's shoulder. It was as if she was making a point and staking her claim on him. 'Hello again.'

Pippa smiled. 'Hello Ava. It was good of you to step in and help us. Thank you.'

Ava patted Oliver's shoulder. 'Anything for Ollie.'

Pippa's smile pulled tight. She returned her attention to Oliver. 'Yes, but I'm not actually ready to go over things yet. I still need those twenty-five minutes. Declan changed the menu and I have to print off new ones.'

Oliver's face clouded. 'He's not causing you more work is he?'

Pippa was quick to shake her head. 'No, it will actually make things simpler for us.'

Oliver nodded. 'Good.'

Pippa pointed to the door leading up to the living quarters above the pub. 'I'd better get the menus changed. I won't be long.'

***

When Pippa reappeared with the new menus, Oliver, Ava, Declan and her Aunt Morgan were sitting around a table in the pub's lounge waiting for her.

Morgan smiled. 'Isn't it lucky we have the lovely Ava here to help us today, Pippa?'

Pippa forced another smile. She could tell by the way her aunt's eyes twinkled that she'd taken a shine to Ava, and Declan was watching her with a smile plastered on his face as if he was smitten too. Was she the only one who hadn't been cast under Ava's spell? 'It is.'

Forty minutes later, after finding it difficult to concentrate while explaining the agenda of the day and the competition, as she tried to ignore the glances Ava was periodically making in Oliver's direction, the meeting was over and it was just minutes until opening time. They could already hear the different tones of dog barking outside, as the owners and their pets waited patiently outside the pub.

Pippa's chest fluttered with nervous excitement as Oliver turned around to look at them all getting ready as he slid back the dead bolts, ready to open the door. 'Ready?'

Pippa nodded. 'Ready.'

Pippa's eyes widened when Oliver opened the door and she saw at least twenty people and a dozen dogs. She saw two terriers, three spaniels, a handful of mixed breed designer dogs, a staffy and a greyhound. She looked past the line of people and saw more cars pulling into the carpark.

She turned to look at her Aunt Morgan who was standing by her side with her pen and clipboard ready to take down entry details. Her aunt handed her the entry numbers to click onto the dogs' collars and smiled. 'Looks like we're in for a busy day.'

***

The competition went above and beyond Pippa's expectations. She looked on as Ava called out the overall winner. There was rapturous applause as the winning dog and its owner walked up to Ava, who proudly presented them with the prize.

Oliver stepped forward with his camera and took a photo of a beaming Ava with the winner, who was the daughter of a neighbouring farm and her sheepdog, an English Shepherd. Bozer the sheepdog had amazed everyone with his tricks, obedience and utter cuteness.

As soon as everything had settled down, there was a rush for the bar. Thankfully. Brett was there behind the bar with Oliver to help out, Morgan was in the kitchen with Declan dishing out bowls of smoked sausage casserole for both the dogs and their owners, and Pippa was the server.

It gave Pippa the first real chance to catch up with the locals she hadn't had a chance to speak to yet, and to thank the competition entrants who'd stayed for a drink and a bite to eat.

Pippa noticed a couple of her friends from school had stayed behind to order food. They waved her over to their table where there were warm long hugs exchanged.

'Pippa, it's so lovely to see you back here. It's not the same just hearing your voice on the other end of a line. I like to see those baby blues, too,' said her friend Mina.

Her other friend Hayley, elbowed Pippa softly in the ribs. 'What's going on? We'd heard Oliver was working here, but we didn't believe it until we saw it with our own eyes.'

Pippa crossed her arms, feigning anger. 'You tell me. How long has he been back in England from America? And why didn't you tell me he was back in the village?'

Mina shot Hayley a knowing smile. 'Told you.'

Pippa looked from one friend to the other. 'Told her what?'

Hayley looked up into Pippa's wide eyes. 'Oliver's been back for six months, but I didn't think you'd be interested. It was only a childhood romance you had...' her brow drew together unsure, '...wasn't it?'

Mina shook her head. 'No. I've told you over the years how much Pippa liked Oliver, Hayley.' She turned from Hayley and looked up at Pippa. 'He broke your heart didn't he Pip? That's why you've never been able to settle into a relationship with anyone else, isn't it?.'

Pippa's jaw dropped open and she put her hands on her hips. 'I can't believe my love life has been *your* topic of conversation in my absence.'

Hayley winked up at Pippa. 'We have to have some entertainment. This village is a ghost of its former self. Remember how nice it was when we were kids?'

Pippa shook her head. 'Never mind that. I want to know why you didn't tell me Oliver was back?'

'Why? You live in Ireland now, anyway. You barely come back and see your family, let alone your best friends. I can't see how the knowledge of him being here would benefit you in any way.' Mina's voice trembled, unable to hide the hurt she was feeling.

Pippa sat on the bench seat next to Mina and slid her arm around her shoulders. 'I'm sorry, Mina.' She looked across at Hayley and extended her hand to her other friend. 'I'm sorry, girls. You know my reasons for moving away to Ireland.'

Hayley reached across and took it. 'Yes, we know. We understood the motivation for the sudden move. We just miss you is all.'

'I miss you, too. Sorry for my little outburst. I think the pressure is getting to me.'

'Pressure? Of working so close to your ex?' winked Hayley.

Pippa laughed. 'What is it with all this winking? Trouble is with you girls, you know me too well.'

Mina's mouth dropped open and she gasped. 'So there is still a flame burning?'

'More like blazing...but I've got stiff competition.' Pippa steered her gaze towards Ava.

Mina and Hayley's eyes followed. 'Really? She has nothing on you. You are a natural beauty. She has more of a fake tan and blonde from a bottle of peroxide sort of beauty.'

Pippa's head snatched around to look at her friends again. 'So you're admitting she's beautiful?'

Hayley shrugged. 'There's no denying she's attractive, but I don't think she's Oliver's type.'

'How do you know what his type is? He's been gone for years.'

'Well, he dated you didn't he?'

'And then dumped me...all because of stupid name calling.'

Mina grimaced. 'So you know about the name calling now? Did Oliver tell you?'

Pippa's mouth dropped open. 'Have you known about it all these years?' Pippa couldn't stop herself from snapping.

Hayley held her hands up in a surrender position. 'Hey! We tried to stop it, and we did a good job too with the girls, but you know what boys are like at that age.'

Pippa shook her head and dropped her face in her hands. 'Sorry girls for biting your heads off again. I just have a lot on my mind at the moment.'

Mina rubbed the small of her back. 'You know we are always here for you, Pip.'

She dropped her hands and nodded with a smile. 'I know.'

Metal clinking against glass drew everyone's attention. Pippa turned to the bar to see her father banging a soon against a wine glass. 'Can I get everyone's attention please!' Pippa shot a glance towards Morgan, but she looked dumbfounded. 'I'd like to thank you all for coming here today. Because there are so many locals in here today, I thought I'd make an announcement...'

Chapter thirteen

'...It is with a heavy heart I need to inform you that due to ill health, I have decided to put the pub and hotel on the market, in order to claim an early retirement. I would really love it if someone from the community could be the next owner, but in reality, I know this might not be the case. If on the off chance anyone here is interested, please come and see either myself or Morgan.'

Pippa was gobsmacked as she watched her father nod once and before turning away from the numerous wide eyes steered towards him, which quickly fell away to look at each other with amazement. Oliver patted her father on the shoulder and leaned in to him to talk as an excited buzz of chatter spread through the pub like wildfire.

'I don't believe it!' said Mina.

'Did you know about this?' asked Hayley.

Pippa's mouth fell open unsure how to answer. 'Aunt Morgan mentioned dad's health hasn't been the greatest lately, and that she was trying to talk him into retiring early. Then this morning when I woke up, she informed me an estate agent was coming to value the property. I'm as shocked by this sudden announcement as you are.'

Pippa got up before her friends could pry more answers from out of her and walked on numb legs towards the bar. She sat down on a bar stool at the end of the bar and studied Oliver and her father who were as thick as thieves with their heads glued together still quietly talking.

Her aunt who was also watching them as keenly as Pippa walked over to her side. 'Before you ask, I didn't know that little speech was going to happen either, but people with this type of dementia often experience heightened emotions, so I suppose it was inevitable.' Morgan's hand rubbed the small of Pippa's back. 'Are you okay?' Pippa turned to look at her aunt and nodded. Morgan's brow pulled together the way it did when she was thinking. 'I wonder if Oliver is voicing his interest?'

Pippa shrugged, unable to find her voice yet. The surprise announcement had really knocked her for six. Now it was out in the open it made it more real, and the thought of her family being severed from the pub felt as if a knife had been thrust into her heart. She knew the dull ache would remain there now forever. She would never be able to wander the rooms of their living quarters and visualise her mother in every room.

Turning her head, she noticed her aunt and her weren't the only ones interested in Brett and Oliver's tête-à-tête. Ava was sitting at a table close to the bar nursing a drink, watching them with as much interest as she was.

Pippa's chest tightened, and she realised this feeling was different from how she felt thinking about losing the pub. This was a pang of jealousy for Ava's continued interest in the man who was an ex for both of them. She quickly analysed her reaction. Was this feeling so strong because she didn't want to see their relationship reignite? If so...why? Was she hoping the same would happen for herself?

***

On the beach with Ginger, Pippa unhooked the lead from his collar and watched him bound towards the surf. She pocketed the lead as she watched him play, remembering she hadn't yet attached the tracker. She must attach it to his collar later and download the app for it.

He father had gone for a lie down immediately after talking to Oliver and he'd disappeared with Ava after closing time, so she and her aunt were none the wiser about their little rendezvous.

She saw a figure at the end of the beach walking two pugs towards the froth of the waves and immediately recognised his lively strides. Holding up her arm, she waved and shouted. 'Ned!'

Ned turned his head in her direction and waved back, before changing directions and heading her way. Pippa glanced towards Ginger. She thought it best to put him back on his lead. He'd been good around Oliver's pet Labrador Jess, but she was a girl. Pippa wasn't so sure how he'd be if Ned had male dogs, even though they were only small.

She pulled out her lead and patted her thighs. 'Ginger...here boy.' Ginger continued to jump over the waves. Pippa glanced Ned's way to see him putting his dogs on their leads. It was owner etiquette to put dogs on leads if they were passing or meeting new dogs; she didn't want Ginger to let her down, or vice versa. She walked towards him. 'Ginger. Come here, boy.' He continued to splash. Pippa had to wade into the surf to grab him. She prised her initiative for putting on her wellingtons instead of her trainers like she usually did when she walked Ginger.

Pippa was leading Ginger out of the waves as Ned walked up to her. 'Hello Pippa. Is he in a rebellious mood?' Ned jutted his chin out towards Ginger.

Pippa blew out the air from her inflated cheeks as she nodded. 'Hello Ned. I think he's a bit excitable being back here in the fresh air. He's never had so much freedom. A quick walk around concrete city is all I've managed of late. I'll feel so guilty when I head back home and drag him away from this natural beauty.'

Pippa watched cautiously as the three dogs looked at each other. Maybe Ned's dogs weren't as friendly as Jess had been with Ginger.

Ned pointed out their tails. 'Don't worry, Pippa. Those quick wags show me all three dogs are happy to meet. The time to worry is when the wag is slow. That means the dog is feeling insecure. Then there's no predicting how the dog might react. I tend to pull my dogs away if I see that.'

Pippa's mouth dropped open. 'Wow, that's amazing, Ned. I should know that really being a dog owner, but I don't think I've invested enough time in research and training since getting Ginger. I think I got him on impulse after losing mom...maybe as a way of filling the vast hole in my heart after she'd gone.'

Ned nodded and smiled. 'I understand, Pip. Has it worked?'

Pippa huffed out a small laugh as she looked down at Ginger lovingly. 'More than I realised Ned.' Ginger and the pugs were now sniffing each other. 'They are lovely. What are their names?'

Ned grinned. 'Laurel and Hardy. They have been like a pair of comedians since they were pups.' Pippa laughed. Ned's grin fell and his brow furrowed. 'Is Brett okay, Pip? I didn't realise his arthritis was as bad as that. He never mentions it when we get together.' Ned shook his head slowly. 'I was shocked at the surprise announcement earlier. He never mentioned selling up either... I hate to admit it, but I'm a little hurt he hasn't confined in me.'

Pippa felt her stomach pinch. She wanted to remain loyal to her father and her aunt by not telling anyone about her father's illness, but she's known Ned all her life, and he looked genuinely sad and worried.

Her hand reached for his upper arm. 'He-he's been diagnosed with dementia, Ned. It was confirmed a couple of years ago, but Aunt Morgan has only just informed me. Dad doesn't even want Nile and me to know about it. Aunt Morgan has only just confided in me. That's why I'm back. I came to help out while she tried to persuade him to sell up and retire. It looks as if she's succeeded.'

Ned's weathered face, the result of a lifetime at sea as part of the lifeboat rescue team drained of all colour. His ruddy red cheeks were now ashen. 'I-I'm shocked.'

'Please don't tell anyone, Ned...or let on you know. I've only told you so that you don't think ill of dad for his surprise actions.'

Ned shook his head vehemently. 'I would never think anything of the sort. Brett is my best mate. I'm-I'm just devastated for him...you and Morgan.'

Pippa tried to swallow past the lump which had miraculously formed in her throat. Ginger had stopped sniffing Oliver and Hardy and was sitting down and looking up at her, as if picking up on the welling emotions bubbling inside her.

'I know. I'm still trying to wrap my head around it. Thankfully though, he started a prescription of medication to slow down the progression of the disease as soon as he found out.'

Ned's lips pursed together and he nodded, 'Good.' He pulled Pippa into his arms and hugged her. 'I'm here for you all day and night, Pippa. Whenever you need me for any reason just call me.'

Pippa fought to stop the tears stinging her eyes from shedding as she answered. 'Thank you, Ned.'

He pulled away abruptly and marched off in the opposite direction, but it wasn't quick enough to hide his own shiny eyes, and the crack in his voice as he called for Oliver and Hardy to follow also betrayed his stoic poker face.

***

Pippa released Ginger's lead, and he ran up the stairs ahead of her to the living quarters above the pub. Inside, Brett and Morgan were at the kitchen table with papers fanned out in front of them. They looked up when Pippa closed the entry door.

Brett smiled and motioned her over. 'Pippa, my darling girl. You're back.' Ginger bounded over to them, wagging his tail. 'Come and sit down. I've got some exciting news.'

Pippa's heart leapt. Had he had news from the hospital? Had they got his dementia diagnosis wrong? She turned her head to look at her aunt. Morgan's face was beaming. Whatever news it was, it was good news.

Morgan patted her hand as Pippa sat down at the table. 'It is good news, Kiddo.'

Pippa looked backward and forwards between her Aunt Morgan and her father. 'Well?'

'Oliver is going to buy the pub and hotel.' Brett's smile enveloped his face as he held her gaze, waiting for Pippa's reaction.

'He is? Is that what you were talking about after the winner was announced?' asked Pippa, hiding the mix of disappointment that the news wasn't something positive about his dementia, but also relieved the pub would be purchased by someone from the community.

Brett nodded. 'Isn't it fantastic that someone from Seagull Bay is going to buy it?'

Morgan reached across the table and patted Brett's hand, too. 'It is. We know Oliver would never change things drastically.'

Pippa nodded her agreement, but then she remembered her conversation with him on the beach. He would need a sleeping partner to be able to afford the business. Would the sleeping partner be as sentimental about the place as Oliver?

Pippa got up and hugged her father. 'It's fantastic news, Dad. Declan has given me a list of supplies to fetch for the evening shift. Can you hold off popping the cork from the champagne bottle at least until I get back?' she pulled away with a wink.

Brett belly laughed. 'There will be no cork popping until he signs the contract, but we'll celebrate with a cup of tea and a slice of cake when you get back. Can you see if you can source some homemade cake from somewhere on your travels? I wished we had a bakery or a tearoom here in Seagull Bay.

I love Katherine's café but I wished she did more sweet than savoury foods.'

Pippa patted her father's beer belly and smiled. 'What? And leave no room for your ale?'

They all laughed. Pippa smiled to herself. The action mimicked what her mother used to do to her father. She hoped she was here with them now, watching on bemused.

'Can you call in on Oliver and give him this? Save me going out?' Morgan handed Pippa a brown envelope.

Pippa took the envelope. 'Sure. Is he expecting whatever this is?'

Morgan shook her head. 'No, it's a copy of last year's turnover and the valuation from the estate agent. I thought he'd like to look everything over so he can see we have nothing to hide.'

Pippa nodded. 'Need anything else while I'm out?'

'Just the cake for later,' said Brett.

'Okay, but I get to choose the flavour,' grinned Pippa.

***

Pippa shifted her weight uncomfortably from foot to foot as she stood at the front door of the house she'd frequented daily over a decade ago. She raised her hand and grabbed the knocker, and lifted it, but she made no attempt to drop it.

She looked down at the brown envelope in her other hand, contemplating posting it through the letterbox, but quickly expelled the thought. There were important documents inside. They needed to be placed directly into Oliver's hands.

The knocked slammed down and Pippa was filled with nostalgia as she remembered the excited feeling she used to get when she came to see Oliver when they were dating back in highschool.

She wondered if his bedroom was still decorated the same. She was surprised they'd kept the family house. According to her friends, Mina and Hayley, Oliver's mum had decided to live elsewhere when his father had taken Oliver to live with him in America and the property had remained empty for years.

The door flung open and it was as if she'd been whipped back in time. Pippa looked up into the face she'd called upon all those years ago. Oliver's beard and moustache were gone. She looked up at his clean-shaven face and her eyes instantly strayed to his mouth. Her chest fluttered. She'd forgotten how full his lips were.

His cologne teased its way up her nostrils, adding a stomach clench to the chest flutter. Her eyes dropped from his lips to take in the rest of him. He was wearing a crisp white shirt, open at the neck by one button. A few strands of dark chest hair peeked out from the top. *That* was a new addition on the Oliver of old. The shirt was tucked into navy blue suit trousers with precision creases pinched down the front of each leg. His feet were adorned in shiny dress shoes that were polished to within an inch of their life.

'Pippa? This is a surprise. I was expecting someone else.

Pippa's head flicked back up and she looked into his almost black eyes, fringed with dark lashes that looked as if they'd tripled in thickness now his beard was gone.

Her arm lifted subconsciously and she handed him the envelope. 'Aunt Morgan asked me to give you this.'

Oliver made no attempt to take it, but stepped aside, opening the door wide. 'Come in.'

Pippa took a step over the threshold and the historically familiar smells and sounds greeted her. The loud ticking of the grandfather clock in the hallway. The mahogany of the antique table next to it.

Jess barked and came trotting into the hall. 'Jess. Hello girl.' Pippa placed the envelope down on the table and went down on her haunches to pet Jess.

Oliver pulled up some slack in his trousers and joined her. 'Some guard dog you are.' Pippa laughed as Jess licked at Oliver's freshly shaved face. 'Jess thinks I'm lunch. She hasn't stopped licking me since I shaved it off. She's never seen me without a beard before.'

'You look great.' Oliver's eyes appeared to twinkle at her comment. She quickly added, 'Going somewhere special?'

'To see my bank manager.'

Pippa rose to her feet and Oliver followed her. 'Yes. Congratulations. I'm genuinely pleased it's you taking on the pub.'

Oliver nodded. 'Thank you.'

'So, you managed to secure a sleeping partner?'

Oliver appeared hesitant to answer. 'Yes.'

A knock on the door cut the conversation short. 'Look, I'll catch up with you later. You are still working at the pub aren't you?' Pippa lifted an eyebrow questioningly as she walked towards the door.

Oliver nodded as he followed and reached around her to open it. 'Yes, of course. We'll speak later.'

He pulled open the door and Pippa leaned back slightly, surprised by his caller. Ava was dressed equally impressive as Oliver in a skirted cream suit. Her hair was teased into its immaculate French twist with not a hair out of place. Pippa eyed her perfect make-up. It looked as if it had been applied by a professional. Had she hired a crew of professional beauticians to come to the hotel each morning to make her look this good while she was in the UK? Pippa made a mental note to ask Lizzy, the hotel housekeeper.

Ava's eyes ran up and down Pippa, displaying a look of distaste. 'Oh, I didn't realise Pippa was coming with us.'

Pippa looked from Ava to Oliver. He pulled at his collar, looking uncomfortable for the first time in his designer shirt that fit him like a glove. He opened his mouth to speak, but Pippa answered before him. 'I'm just delivering paperwork.' She stepped past Ava and glanced over her shoulder as she walked down the stone path to the short distance towards the gate. 'I'll see you later, Oliver.'

She couldn't get away from there quick enough. Her stomach had become a coiled knot. Oliver had told her he was going to see the bank manager. He hadn't been expecting to see her because he was expecting Ava. She'd turned up to go with him. Were they dating again? Friends didn't accompany friends to appointments as important as seeing the bank manager—only people in very close relationships did that together.

Pippa still wasn't thinking straight when she walked into Katherine's café trying to hunt down homemade cake to celebrate the selling of the pub with her father and aunt when she got back.

The tinkle of the bell introduced her arrival to Katherine, who appeared from the kitchen just out of sight of the counter. Pippa watched as she secretly tried to dab away tears, before lifting up the corners of her mouth to form the cheery smile she usually greeted customers with.

'Hello Pippa my dear. What can I get you?'

'Do you have any homemade cake by any chance, Katherine?'

Katherine closed her eyes as if trying to recall. She shook her head and opened her eyes. Pippa noticed the quick motion had helped her regain her composure again. She shook her head. 'No sorry love, I've always had more breakfast trade than anything past midday so cakes are not something I've put much effort into.'

Pippa nodded with a smile. 'No worries, thank you anyway.' She began to turn away, but stopped herself. 'Are you alright Katherine?'

Pippa didn't know if it was the soft tone of her voice but Katherine's bottom lip began to quiver. 'I have to move away back to Portsmouth to take care of my elderly mother. She's ninety-four and has been fiercely independent all her life, bless her, but she had the flu recently and it developed into pneumonia. Since then, she's never really recovered. I'm going to have to leave Seagull Bay and move back to care for her. Trouble is, I can't afford not to earn a wage from here. I don't need anything huge, just enough to pay the bills. I'll no doubt have to claim carer's allowance to make up the loss in wages, but you know how this government is. They'll put it in one hand and take it out of the other, one way or another...I'll probably be worse off.'

'I am sorry to hear that, Katherine. You'll be greatly missed. Everyone I speak to has nothing but good praises for you.' Pippa chewed her bottom lip as she thought. 'What if you rent this place? The new tenant can pay their own bills and rent money, but all profit will obviously be their own.'

'I did contemplate something similar, Pippa, but I haven't had a chance to do anything about it yet. Do you think anyone would be interested, though? I only have a week or so to sort everything out before I need to go.'

Pippa held the palms of her hands up. 'What is there to sort out other than a rental agreement? The kitchen is prepped to go. You have all the furniture and utensils in place. The rental can be for a fully furnished café. Why don't you ring up the local estate agents now and explain the sort of contract you need? I'm sure they'll either be able to do it for you or point you in the right direction of someone in the know?'

Katherine's demeanour instantly brightened. 'You are a treasure, Pippa. Thank you.'

Pippa smiled, her low mood now lifted. She'd push Oliver Oney and Ava out of her mind and go back, eat cake and drink tea with her dad and aunt and think of it as the flesh and blood of Christ.

To her it would symbolise rebirth and be the catalyst to reinstall the values she was raised with. She'd put jealousy out of her mind and she'd concentrate on channelling her love into her remaining family to ensure their happiness in the next stage of their life.

She'd work alongside Oliver with a smile on her face for as long as it took. Maybe it was time for her to realise *he was* the one who got away because he wasn't meant for her. He was meant for Ava.

Chapter fourteen

It had been four days since the competition. Pippa had tried her best to push all signs of jealousy out of her heart, but she had found it more difficult than she had realised. Ava had sat at the end of the bar every night, claiming one seat in particular as her own.

Pippa had done her best to chat amicably with her but she had gravitated to helping Declan out more and more in the kitchen, even though she suspected she was getting under his feet, yet Declan was always too polite to say so. But she'd needed to get away from the sickly sweet rapport sizzling between Oliver and Ava.

She'd avoided walking on the beach with Ginger at the same time as Oliver and Jess and had taken to exploring and reacquainting herself with more of the town's steep streets lined with the colourful houses of Seagull Bay, the streets she'd grown up playing tag in with Mina and Hayley.

This morning she was going with Declan to view the little flat above Katherine's café. A chance conversation after calling in on her to enquire about how things were going letting her shop and brought up the flat above it. According to Katherine, the estate agents said they would be able to rent it too, but it needed substantial work to renovate it first, something she had no time to do as she was a week away from moving back to Portsmouth to care for her mother. In fact, Katherine had stated she'd see how things were, but she might even be forced to rent out her house at a later stage too.

COMING HOME TO SEAGULL BAY

Pippa bounced down the steps leading from the living quarters and headed for the side door, where she said she'd meet Declan. He was still sitting on his motorbike with his crash helmet on. Pippa couldn't deny he looked an impressive sight in his leather jacket with the sun gleaming off the chrome exhaust pipe and reflective black paintwork. He waved to her when he spotted her.

'Morning Pippa. Thanks for doing this with me. I just need a second pair of eyes to ensure it's going to be big enough for me and my pup. He's a big dog and he needs space, but I'm so desperate to get out of the house I'm sharing with my friend at the moment. In my state of mind, I'll take a matchbox to live in. But we both know that wouldn't be good for a St Bernard.'

Pippa laughed. 'Don't worry. I'll be your common sense friend for the day.'

Pippa couldn't see his mouth, but by the way his eyes were crinkling up, she knew Declan was smiling. 'Thank you.' He held up another helmet she'd failed to notice. 'As a thank you, we'll ride to the flat and after we've viewed it, I'll take you for a spin over the moors as a way of saying thanks.'

Pippa gasped, and then her mouth curled up into a smile, spreading from ear to ear. She stepped forward and took the helmet. 'How do I put it on?'

'Hold on to the straps and give it a good tug down, then I'll fasten the strap for you.'

Pippa did as she was instructed and as Declan was fastening the strap, Oliver came walking towards them.

'You're not taking Pippa on that thing are you?'

Pippa was shocked by his rude assault with not so much as a good morning first. Oliver turned around to defend himself.

'Yes. I'm a proficient rider. I've been riding a bike for fifteen years. Pippa will be perfectly safe with me.'

Oliver's eyes were hooded by his frown, and anger fumed from them. He looked from Declan to Pippa. 'You can't seriously be thinking of going on that thing.'

Pippa could feel her anger bubbling inside her. Oliver had spent every spare minute he'd had in the last four days with Ava. She'd even extended her stay here. Not that Pippa had found out from Oliver. She only knew because of Ava booking additional nights at the hotel. So much for continuing with their friendship. He hadn't even had the courtesy to tell her when they'd been having a rare catch up with each other before opening up days ago.

Pippa recalled how awkward it had been. Both of them had skirted around how the paperwork regarding the sale was going. The main topic of conversation had been their beloved pets.

Pippa held Oliver's gaze and crossed her arms defensively. 'Yes, I am...not that it's any concern of yours. I'm sure you have other things to worry about. Like the takeover of my family's pub and whether you are adding too much soda to Ava's numerous wines spritzers.'

Oliver's jaw dropped and Pippa took the opportunity to straddle her leg over the bike and pull herself ungracefully on behind Declan.

He swivelled around and pointed to the footrests. 'You could have used those to climb on. Put your feet on them and hold on tight!'

With that, the engine fired up, and Declan pulled back the throttle, revving up the engine. Oliver staggered back a couple of steps, snapping his mouth shut. His chin jutted out and Pippa noticed his hands clench by his sides. Her heart raced with excitement and fear. Declan pulled away and she turned her head to watch Oliver storm away with his shirt pulling taut across his wide shoulders.

Pippa tried to enjoy the short journey over the beachfront to Katherine's café, but the tight ball in the pit of her stomach made the ride forgettable.

Katherine was waiting in front of the café when they pulled to a stop less than a minute later. Her dazzling smile made Pippa put her own worries to one side and concentrate her efforts on helping Declan with his plight to find a home. Declan turned the engine off and began to unfasten his chin strap.

Pippa dismounted the bike easier than she'd climbed on and fiddled with the unfastening of her helmet as Declan put the side stand down. She offered Katherine a genuine smile. 'Morning Katherine.'

'Good morning my lovelies.' Katherine turned her attention to Declan. 'Oh Declan, it's such a mess up there. I wished I'd taken the tome to fix it up. I feel awful. Are you sure you want to view it?'

Declan laughed. 'Are you trying to talk me or yourself out of this?'

'Goodness no. I need to rent the flat, and sooner rather than later. It's just, I'll feel bad if you want it because you'll have to do a lot of work getting it to a decent living state before you can move in.'

'It just means I'll appreciate it all the more when I'm living there.'

Katherine shook her head with a smile. 'I'll tell you what. If this is the place for you, I'll let you have it for half price for the first two months while you do it up.'

'Wow. That's extremely generous of you, Katherine. Excellent, lead the way.' Oliver held out his arm, gesturing for Katherine to go first.

Pippa followed at the rear as Katherine led the way around the back of the café to a side door.

The stairs leading up to the flat were void of carpet and the wallpaper lining the walls was peeling off. Katherine turned around to look at Declan and Pippa with a grimace. She continued up the stairs. Pippa noticed it smelled like stale air, but she didn't detect any residual mould. That was a good sign, at least.

The door at the top of the stairs used to be white, but now it had yellowed with age. It opened into quite a spacious sitting room with two small curtainless windows letting in lots of light. This room was the full width of the building and had half the wallpaper scraped off, appearing as if someone had made a halfhearted attempt to re-decorate. The floor was also carpetless and there were a few floorboards missing and copper pipes exposed.

Katherine held her hand out. 'Be careful. As you can see there are missing floorboards but I don't know where they are. I think the previous owner must have thrown them away.'

Declan stepped past Katherine and turned his head from left to right as he surveyed the room. He turned back with an ecstatic grin. 'That is no problem to fix.' Declan turned to Pippa. 'What do you think so far?'

Pippa nodded her head. 'Spacious.'

'Unfortunately, this isn't the worst room, Declan.' Katherine continued into the kitchen. 'There are no cabinets in here.'

A sink was plumbed in, but it rested on a two wooden boxes which were taking its weight. Pippa glanced at Declan, but the smile he'd held in the sitting room was still blazing on his lips. He nodded. 'Okay. A little more challenging, but still doable.'

Pippa was being drawn along by Declan's positivity, her job as the common sense friend going out the window.

Katherine led them through to the bathroom, which was very small, but other than needing a good scrub, was in perfect order. 'Just a little elbow grease is needed in here.' She led them into the final room, the bedroom. 'And like the rest of the flat, this room just needs decorating.'

Declan beamed at Pippa and Pippa beamed back, nodding her head. 'Yes, I like it. I'll help you with the decorating and you can do the manual work.'

Declan turned to Katherine. 'You did say that you allow pets didn't you?'

Katherine nodded. 'Oh course I do. This is a pet friendly property.'

Declan held out his hand. 'I'll take it, Katherine, thank you.'

Pippa clenched her hands into triumphant fists and raised them in the air. 'Yayyy.'

***

Ten minutes later, Pippa was once again a pillion passenger on the back of Declan's bike as they headed up the hill, taking them out of Seagull Bay up onto the main road.

The wind blew in through the vents of the helmet, and Pippa inhaled deeply. It was cold but exhilarating as it filled her lungs and she was glad she'd dressed in jeans and a sweater that morning. Her jacket was zipped up to her neck and her hands were cozy warm in the leather gloves Declan had handed her outside the café as they'd said their goodbyes to Katherine.

They were soon up in the North York Moors whizzing through the beautiful scenery. All that was missing from the picturesque scenes were the patches of purple heather that bloomed in abundance come August. Her chest tightened. Would she see them this year? Now the pub was sold and her father was retiring, there was no need for her to stay—especially now that Oliver had rekindled his relationship with Ava. Ginger would miss living by the sea, but what could she do?

Her thoughts turned to Oliver, and his reaction to her taking a ride on Declan's bike. It had taken her by surprise. Had his concern been for her safety? Or was it because it was Declan and not him she would be sitting behind and hugging tightly onto? Who was she trying to fool? Oliver loved Ava and she loved Declan, but not in that way. He was definitely in the friend zone. Declan reminded her so much of her brother, Nile. In fact, she was finding herself hanging out with Declan more and more because she missed her brother so much, something she'd never admit out loud to Nile.

Did Oliver love Ava? Only last week Declan had commented on how he thought Oliver was into her after he'd acted weird when she'd first met Declan outside the pub. Declan must have got it wrong.

The bike slowed down and Declan pulled into a layby at the top of a hill and turned off the engine. He tapped her leg, indicating for her to dismount. Pippa did it correctly that time using the foot pegs to climb off the bike.

Declan pulled down the side stand and took off his helmet. He pointed out to the moor in front of them. 'This is my spot. This is where I come to think, and if I can borrow the use of a car, bring my pup too for a long walk.'

Pippa removed her helmet and stepped up to his side to admire the view. 'It's beautiful. I bet you've solved many a problem up here.'

Declan nodded. 'Yes, I have. That's why I've brought you here now. Don't think I haven't noticed you brooding this last week.'

People turned her head to look at him to find him studying her profile. 'What do you mean?'

Declan smiled a kind smile, but Pippa swore it masked pity. 'I've seen how Ava's constant presence in the pub is affecting you. The torch you're carrying for Oliver hasn't extinguished you know.'

Pippa's mouth dropped open. 'I-I don't carry a torch for him.'

'And I'm a secret billionaire.'

Pippa closed her eyes, tilted her head back and puffed out of inflated cheeks. 'Ugh, is it that obvious?' She looked up into his kind blue eyes. 'What do I do Declan? He's resumed his relationship with Ava.'

'Has he though?'

Pippa's brow knitted together. 'What do you mean?'

'Have you ever seen them hold hands, steal loving glances...or even kiss?'

Pippa looked down at the ground and thought hard. She looked back at Declan and shook her head. 'No.'

'Neither have I, and I've seen them walking through Seagull Bay together and part company without so much as a peck on the cheek. Surely, if they were in a romantic relationship, there would be some kind of physical touch. A hand placed lovingly on the small of her back... Pushing a lock of hair away from her cheek?'

Pippa's cheeks heated as she remembered the numerous times Oliver had done those things to her—before Ava came on the scene.

Pippa shook her head slowly. 'I-I don't know Declan. Why has she extended her stay here?'

'Business? Isn't that what she came to England for?'

'Yes, that and to catch up with Oliver.'

'Why don't you ask him?'

Pippa baulked. 'What?'

'Invite Oliver for a morning walk on the beach again with your dogs. You told me you haven't been on a walk with him in days. Invite him on one after the lunchtime shift.' Pippa bite her bottom lip unsure. 'Think of Ginger. He'd love to see Jess again.'

Pippa crossed her arms and tried to stop the smile snaking across her lips. 'Using blackmail to pull at my heartstrings is a bit low, Declan.'

'But it's working, isn't it? I can already see your mind ticking away behind those green eyes of yours, planning how you are going to ask him.'

Pippa nodded with a smirk and looked out at the luscious view again. 'You're right. This place helps...I'll be coming here again.'

***

Pippa's stomach was a flutter all throughout the lunchtime rush. It was busier on the bar than in the kitchen and even though she'd wanted to hide away with Declan in the kitchen, she'd been forced by the need to help Oliver behind the bar.

Thankfully, Ava rarely came in at lunchtimes and so the crackling tension Pippa thought had been lost between them, which appeared to be on top form today, was only apparent to her...or so she thought until Reverend Townsend popped into the pub.

'Good afternoon to you two lovebirds. I heard the doggy competition was a real success. But I also heard that Brett is selling up. I really hope the new owner will continue hosting the competition.' He laughed and shook his head. 'Meals served in dog bowls—genius idea.'

Pippa pointed a finger between Oliver and herself. 'We're not a couple, Reverend Townsend...remember us telling you on the beach.'

The Reverend frowned. 'Yes, I remember. It's just that—' he shook his head, '—never mind... Is Brett about?'

'He's out with Aunt Morgan.'

The Reverend tapped the counter of the bar and smiled ethereally. 'Never mind. I'll call back later.' He winked. 'It will give me an excuse to sneak a pint of beer.' He turned away from them and waved a backward wave. 'Cheerio.'

Pippa and Oliver looked at each other and burst into fits of giggles. It was the tension breaking moment Pippa had wished for all lunchtime. 'What are you up to after this shift?'

'I'm going to the estate agents.' Pippa tried not to let her disappointment show on her face, but she'd never had a very good poker one. 'Why?'

She shrugged. 'Oh, I just thought it would be nice for Jess and Ginger to meet up for a walk again.'

'I'll go tomorrow instead.'

Pippa nodded. 'That's great. Shall I meet you on the beach at eight?'

Oliver's mouth twisted into a grin, and he shook his head. 'No. I mean I'll go to the estate agents tomorrow. Jess would love to meet up with Ginger. She's been cooped up for days. I've been so busy I'm afraid to admit I've slightly neglected her.'

'You should have said. I'd have been more than happy to take her for a walk with Ginger.'

Oliver cocked his chin towards the door leading into the kitchen. 'I thought you were too pre-occupied.' Pippa's mouth dropped open. Oliver shook his head. 'Sorry. I didn't mean that. I-I just have a lot on my mind, trying to get things in order to buy this place.'

Pippa shook her head. 'It's fine.' Her heart was thudding at twice the speed it was a minute ago. Had she been mistaken, or had Oliver just shown he was jealous of her spending time with Declan? 'Shall I meet you on the beach at four?'

Oliver nodded with a thin-lipped smile. 'Yes, I'll bring a couple of balls.'

Pippa's cheeks heated. She was glad he wasn't a mind reader. Only God was privy to the vision that just flashed in her mind.

***

Dusk was quickly drawing in when Jess came bounding down the beach, barking excitedly when she spotted Ginger frolicking in the surf. Ginger stopped what he was doing when he heard her and raced at full speed towards her. They greeted each other momentarily before racing off doing zoomies. Pippa looked on with an enormous grin. How could she have kept her beloved pet from seeing his friend? Their time on Earth was preciously short as it was.

Oliver joined her as she watched them run together along the shoreline. 'Here.' Pippa looked down to see him handing her a ball. She took it and their hands briefly touched. She instantly experienced the tingle of electric she read about in her romance novels. 'Shall we walk?'

'Yes.' They strolled side-by-side in silence for the first five minutes, watching their pets. It was Pippa's burning curiosity that broke the silence. 'Estate agents? Is that to do with the pub?'

Oliver glanced her way and then looked off into the distance. Pippa studied his profile. She could see his jaw was still as square as when he was in high school now his beard was gone.

'I don't want to, but I'm contemplating selling the house. Mom and dad gave it to me, but it's the only way of securing the pub without using the sleeping partner I've obtained... My gut is telling me even though promises have been made to not change anything, I think the prospective partner has other ideas.'

Pippa gasped and her hand flew to her mouth. 'Oh no.'

Oliver sunk his face into his hands. 'I know. I'm stuck between a rock and a hard place. Selling my family home is the last thing I want to do. I want to be able to secure the pub without it. I have the option to go with the sleeping partner, but there's no saying she won't change things because she said she wouldn't sign anything giving me one-hundred percent control over the say of how things are run.'

Pippa bristled. 'She?'

Oliver nodded. 'Yes...Ava.'

Chapter fifteen

Pippa regretted storming off the beach—regretted it because she'd left without uttering a reason why she was leaving Oliver, and because she'd pulled Ginger away from Jess. Oliver had called after her, but she hadn't answered him. She couldn't trust her mouth not saying the words her mind was thinking. She'd been thankful that Ginger had for once come to her on the first command. He must have sensed she was upset. Geez she loved that dog.

After that, she couldn't face Oliver again. That meant no more working in the pub. She felt selfish and awful about letting her aunt down, but she just couldn't face him. So she'd hidden away in her bedroom the following day, saying she wasn't up to it when her father had knocked on the door, asking if she was going down to work the pub late morning. She was surprised when her father hadn't pushed her for a reason.

Instead, she'd decided to busy herself getting the decorating supplies together to help Declan in his flat after he'd given her free rein to do as she wanted as long as the colour pink wasn't involved.

As she headed for Old Po's, she bumped into her high school friend, Mina. 'I was just on my way to see you.'

'No work today?'

Mina shook her head and winked. 'That's what I was coming to find out from you.'

Pippa frowned. 'Has my Aunt Morgan been on the phone with you this morning by any chance?'

'She's only worried. She heard you leave as she was heading to your room to talk to you.' Pippa sighed. 'What's up Pippa Pickles?'

Pippa lifted her eyebrows and tilted her head in warning. 'Don't. I'm not in the mood.'

Mina pulled a mock grimace. 'Must be bad.'

Pippa rolled her eyes and shook her head. 'Fancy helping me pick out some paint and wallpaper for Declan?' Mina screwed up her face. 'We can talk.' Pippa baited her, feeling as if she wouldn't mind unloading some of the weight on her shoulders after all.

Mina slipped her arm through Pippa's. 'Where we off to? Old Po's?'

'Yup.'

'Fantastic. I love that shop. It's like time stood still in there. It's exactly the same as I remembered it being from when I was a kid. I think it even has the same cobwebs.'

Pippa laughed and threw her head back. Spending time with Mina was just the tonic she needed.

***

It turned out they couldn't talk freely in Old Po's as nosey Mrs Calloway was in there wagging Old Po's ear off.

Pippa and Mina settled for subtle greys and calming modern blues. They grabbed what they could carry and Pippa made arrangements to collect the other decorating supplies before closing time.

Weighed down with tins of paint, sandpaper and paintbrushes, they walked the cobbled steep streets, heading for Katherine's café and the flat above it.

'Okay, spill your guts!' Pippa spluttered a laugh at Mina's comment. 'Not literally.'

Pippa caught her breath. 'Ugh, where do I begin?'

'Just start with why you haven't worked in the pub today.'

Pippa sucked in a big breath. 'It's because I was walking on the beach yesterday with Oliver and the dogs—*the first time in days might I add*—and he said something that made me so mad, I had to get out of there before I said something I might have regretted.'

'Which was?'

'He alluded that Ava was his sleeping partner.'

Mina's eyes and mouth opened wide. 'Oliver is sleeping with the American?'

Pippa looked at her friend, her brow furrowed as she shook her head. 'No Mina.' She banged the heel of her hand on her forehead. 'I forgot to tell you—sorry. Oliver is buying the pub, but he can't afford it on his own, so he's securing a sleeping partner to fund part of the money for it.'

'Ah, okay. And you think the sleeping partner is Ava...why?'

'Because he said *she* when he was talking about the partner yesterday. He more or less told me he either has to sell his family home or he'd have to use the sleeping partner he'd secured. But he was wary because he wasn't sure she wouldn't change things in the pub.'

Mina's mouth dropped open and she covered it with her hand. 'OMG Pippa, it didn't click until you told me that, but I saw Mr Herbert's car parked outside Oliver's house on my way to your house.'

'And Mr Herbert is who?'

'He's the new owner of Bricks and Mortar.'

'Who is that?'

'It's the estate agents from the high street above Seagull Bay.'

They'd reached the side door at Kathrine's café—Declan's front door to his new flat. Pippa put the supplies she was carrying down.

'Do you think this means he's decided to sell his house and not have the American as his sleeping partner?' asked Mina.

Pippa instantly felt nauseous. Had her appalling behaviour on the beach swayed his decision? She decided she must go and speak to him as soon as the lunchtime shift had finished. For the time being, she'd channel all of her nervous energy into decorating Declan's flat.

***

As Pippa neared the pub, she thought she'd better let Ginger out before she went into the pub to speak to Oliver before he locked up after the lunchtime shift, because due to her selfishness, her poor father and aunt would have had to work today.

She let herself in through the side door and quickly jogged up the stairs. Opening the front door, she was expecting Ginger to jump up her, excited to see her, but he didn't. 'Ginger, here boy.' She looked around the door to where she hung up his lead, but it was still on the peg.

Her stomach pinched, suddenly frightened in case he was ill. She rushed into the open plan sitting room and looked down to where he usually slept. His daybed was empty. Rushing from the sitting room, she made her way down the hall to her bedroom. She flung the door open, but he wasn't in there either. Pippa went from room to room, but he wasn't anywhere in the living quarters.

She took a deep breath. She was panicking unnecessarily. Her aunt must have taken him downstairs into the pub so he wouldn't be on his own all morning. It was a dog friendly pub after all.

Making her way downstairs, she looked down at herself before she entered the door which would open up into the pub. She looked a state. She had blobs of paint stained all over her clothes. She silently cursed Mina under her breath for the two-minute paintbrush flicking contest she provoked her into. Thankfully, all the customers would be gone by now. There would only be Aunt Morgan, her father, Declan and...Oliver in there. She puffed out her cheeks, which were already red at the thought of him seeing her in that state.

Oliver had his back to her putting away the dry glasses from the dishwasher and Brett was sitting at the end of the bar, sipping a coffee. His face brightened when he saw Pippa. 'Here's my princess. What have you been up to Pip?'

Oliver swung around to look at her, his eyes racking her clothing and his brow pulling into a frown.

'Erm, decorating Declan's new flat.' She watched Oliver through the corner of her eye. His tense body language indicated he didn't like her answer. She looked around for her pet. 'Where Ginger, Dad?'

Brett pointed up to the ceiling. 'Upstairs in the house, isn't he?'

Pippa's heart shot up into her throat. She rushed towards the kitchen and heard Oliver speak before she pushed open the door. 'Was he there when you came down this morning, Brett?'

'Yes, I believe so.'

'Aunt, have you seen Ginger? He's not upstairs, but he was there when I left this morning.'

Morgan and Declan spun around on hearing Pippa's voice. Her aunt's brow lifted with surprise. 'He was upstairs when I came down.' Her lifted brow dropped and pulled together. 'He was in the house with Brett.' Pippa's hand flew to her mouth. 'Use the new tracker you have.'

A breeze behind her indicated the door was closing. Someone had come in from the bar.

Pippa shook her head. 'I-I never attached the tag to his collar.'

Her aunt rushed forward. 'I did...this morning. I saw it laying on the mantelpiece so I clipped it on.'

Oliver appeared at her side. 'Download the app. We can track him down immediately.'

Pippa pulled the phone from her back pocketed of her jeans. Her hands were trembling as she unlocked her phone. 'I-I can't stop shaking.'

'Here, let me do it for you.' Oliver took the phone from her hands and expertly flipped through the screens.'

'Is there anything I can do?' asked Declan.

Morgan looked over her shoulder at him. 'Can you go with them? Three sets of eyes are better than two.' Pippa noticed Oliver glance up from the phone at her aunt's suggestion. 'Brett and I will stay here in case he comes back and scratches at the door to be let in.'

Oliver turned the phone around to show the screen to Pippa. 'I don't believe it. It appears he's somewhere close to my house.' He passed the phone to Pippa. 'Come on, let's go.'

Pippa, Oliver and Declan raced from the kitchen, through the lounge, and out of the pub. Oliver's house was located at the top of Steep Street and Pippa was relieved when he headed for the quick way they used to take when they were teenagers, through the narrow alleyways at the back of the small gardens, which were everywhere around Seagull Bay giving access to residents whose dwellings were behind the main streets, walked daily by the many tourists attracted to the small seaside town.

The tension in her shoulders only got worse the closer they got, and it didn't help that there was also tension radiating from Oliver towards Declan, either.

Nearing the alley that lead out onto Steep Street, Declan spoke for the first time since leaving The Cheese Wedge and Pickles. 'Check the app again Pippa, to see if he's moved.'

Pippa stopped walking, quickly tapped in the numbers to unlock her screen. The app tab was still open and she studied the screen. 'He's moving, but he's still somewhere at the top of Steep Street.'

'Let's spread out,' said Oliver.

They emerged from the alley and set off in different directions all calling out Ginger's name.

Pippa grimaced as she watched Oliver and Declan calling simultaneously, both loud—as if competing with each other. She was worried about their over enthusiastic shouting scaring

Ginger away. She stared down at the screen and concentrated on her own search.

The red blip which represented Ginger had started to move erratically. She gritted her teeth. She was right. He was getting spooked. He would already be frightened alone in a place he didn't know.

'I've found him!' shouted Declan. Pippa felt as if a boulder had been lifted from her shoulders. 'I'm over here by number fifteen. I'll wait here.'

He was right by Oliver's house. Pippa quickly made her way from out of an alley she'd been searching back onto Steep Street. Declan was on his haunches with his hand held firmly on Ginger's collar, while stroking him. Oliver appeared from the back of number nineteen with a perplexed look. If Pippa didn't know any better, she'd swear he was jealous.

Pippa rushed over to Ginger. 'Ginger! Oh my days, you scared mommy so much. Thank goodness you are alright.' Ginger barked, excited to see Pippa. She wrapped her arms around him and kissed the top of his head more times than she could count. Ginger wriggled in her arms enough to lift his snout and lick her face.

'Well done.' Oliver said as he looked down at Declan.

Pippa lifted her face from Ginger and beamed at Declan. 'Yes, thank you Declan.'

Declan shook his head. 'Anyone of us could have spotted him. I'm just glad he's unhurt.'

Pippa's hands flew to her cheeks. 'Oh no, I should have grabbed his lead.'

'Don't worry, I got this.' Oliver bent down and slid his hands underneath Ginger and lifted him with ease.

It was only then that Pippa noticed the for sale sign post outside Oliver's family home.

They walked down the hilly street, taking the long route. Pippa couldn't keep the smile from off her face as she looked up at her beloved pet, but she also felt a little sad after seeing the sign.

***

Aunt Morgan was pacing outside the pub with her walking stick tapping on the cobbles and a face wretched with worry lines. She turned to face them as they approached, but only a few of the lines disappeared with her small smile of relief when she saw Ginger safe and well in Oliver's arms. Pippa's gut tightened. She knew by her aunt's diluted reaction to Ginger's return there was something much greater troubling her.

'What's wrong Aunt?'

Morgan rushed forward. 'It's your father. He was muttering that Ginger's disappearance was all his fault. He said he must have let him out to pee and forgot about him... He rushed out to go and look for him.' Morgan grabbed Pippa's hands and her eyes sought Pippa's and her voice trembled. 'He's not good when he's mithered like this, Pippa. His condition worsens. I'm so worried.'

'Condition? His arthritis?' asked Oliver.

Pippa turned to Oliver, her eyes going from him to Declan. She glanced back at her aunt and Morgan nodded, giving permission to tell all. Pippa looked at Oliver again. 'He has dementia. He didn't want anyone to know.'

Morgan piped in. 'Emotions can become extremely heightened at times. So if he's feeling guilty, the emotion will be amplified.'

'Or if he's scared,' said Pippa, turning back to face her aunt with wide eyes.

'I'll call Ned. He might know where he's gone,' said Morgan.

Pippa reached forward and grabbed her aunt's arm. 'Ned knows, Aunt...I-I had to confide in someone.'

Morgan swapped her walking stick into her other hand so she could squeeze Pippa's hand. 'It's okay. Brett was planning on telling you and Nile and his friends, anyway. It's better if everyone knows.' Pippa nodded. 'I'll go and make that call.'

Morgan went into the pub and Pippa turned to face Oliver and Declan. 'Let's get Ginger in the pub and then if you don't mind. Can you help me search for dad?'

Oliver's face softened. 'Of course.'

Declan nodded. 'I'll go now. I'll start on the south side of Seagull Bay.'

'Thanks Declan.'

Declan turned around and ran off in that direction. Ginger whimpered in Oliver's arms. 'Come on Boy, let's get you settled. I think you've had enough adventure for today,' said Oliver.

'Do you think he was trying to find Jess?' asked Pippa.

'He's a smart fellow, so maybe.'

Pippa unlocked the side door and ran up the stairs ahead of Oliver to open the door leading into the house above the pub. She filled a fresh bowl of water and tipped some kibble in his bowl, and they both fussed over him for a few minutes.

Pippa turned to look at Oliver. 'Shall we go and see what Ned's said before we start our search?'

'Good idea.'

***

Morgan was at the foot of the stairs as they were about to descend them. 'I was just coming to let you know what's happening. Ned's ringing around the community letting everyone know the situation. They're all going to be on the lookout for him.'

Pippa and Oliver swiftly descended the stairs and stood in front of Morgan.

Pippa nodded and exhaled a deep breath of relief. 'It's good to know the community is still ready to rally their support in times of crisis.' Oliver nodded in agreement. She looked up into his eyes, hers steely with determination. 'Ready?'

Oliver nodded. 'Yes. Let's go find your father.'

***

They naturally stayed together and gravitated towards the streets near the beach. Pippa didn't know how worried to feel. There was no denying her father had dementia. His small lapses in memory were the proof she'd seen since she'd been back home, but apart from that, he appeared to be fully compos mentis. He was out looking for Ginger, so maybe they were all being overly cautious. Pippa really hoped she was right.

The silence was lengthening between them, and although not opportune, Pippa thought this was the perfect time to talk to Oliver.

'Ollie?' He turned to look at her profile. She knew that would get his attention. 'I don't want you to put your family home on the market.'

He stopped walking and turned to look at her with a frown. 'Are you saying you want me to accept Ava as my sleeping partner, because it's too late for that now? After your reaction yesterday, I've already told her I've decided to go it alone. Right about now, she'll be landing back in LA airport.'

Pippa knew she'd been right guessing it was Ava. She turned to look at him and shook her head. 'No. What I'm trying to tell you is...*I'd* like to be your partner.' His face lit up. 'I mean your sleeping partner. I've done a quick calculation and worked out if I sell my apartment in Ireland, and then if needs must, get a small loan if I fall short, I'll be able to match what Ava would have contributed.'

Pippa was shocked when Oliver turned his back on her. Had his rejection of the offer been so immediate? Pippa's stomach dropped into her feet when he shook his head, confirming her intuition.

'No.' She felt as if she'd been stabbed in the chest. 'No,' he repeated. He spun around to face her, his eyes staring intensely at her. Her heart pounded in her chest. He looked wild with anger at her suggestion. 'No...I don't want you as my sleeping partner, Pippa...I want you as my...partner in life. I want you to be my wife.' He took a step towards her. The wild look Pippa had mistaken for anger was love.

'W-what?'

He cupped her face in his hands. 'You were the one who got away Pippa.' Pippa gasped. Oliver got down on one knee and Pippa choked back a sob. This was the reoccurring dream she'd had her whole life. Oliver searched the sand around him until he spotted a length of twine. He grabbed it and pulled something out of his pocket. It was his penknife. He flicked it open.

'What are you going to do with that?'

Oliver looked up with a grin and a gleam in his eye. 'Once a Seagull Bay kid, always a Seagull Bay kid.' He cut the string, tied it into a small hoop and pocked the knife. He held up the string hoop and grabbed Pippa's hand, searching her eyes as he spoke. 'Pippa Pickles.' Pippa let out a half sob, half chuckle. 'Will you give me the honour of accepting my marriage proposal? Will you be my wife?'

The tears that had swiftly gathered on her lower lashes as Pippa had watched Oliver fashion a string engagement ring, now ran freely down her cheeks.

'Yes. Yes, of course I will Oliver Onions. Then if we're lucky enough to have children one day, they'll be our little pickled onions.'

Oliver laughed and slid the string onto Pippa's finger. He jumped to his feet and took her in his arms. Pippa stared up into his brown eyes, drowning in the dark pools. He lowered his mouth to hers and his soft lips kissed her again for the first time in years. Pippa's heart swelled. It was as if she were fifteen again.

Her phone began to ring and she reluctantly pulled away. She fished it out of her pocket and stared down at the screen. Her aunt's named flashed on the screen. Pippa's heart palpitated in her chest. She hoped it was good news. She answered and put the call on loudspeaker for Oliver to hear.

'Pippa...He's been found.'

Pippa let out the breath she didn't realise she'd been holding in. 'Oh thank goodness. Where?'

'Ned remembered a place they used to hang out when they were kids. He was there, sitting down, looking out at the sea. When Ned asked him if he'd been out looking for Ginger, Ned said he looked shocked and said, 'Ginger is missing?' Bless him, he'd forgotten he'd gone out searching for him... Anyway, he's home safe now.'

Oliver's face showed the relief Pippa was feeling. 'Okay Aunt, we're coming back now.'

***

Back in the pub, Brett, Ned and Morgan were sitting at the bar. Oliver and Pippa walked in holding hands. As soon as Morgan noticed their entwined fingers, she smiled.

Pippa went straight over to her father and wrapped her arms around his neck. 'You scared me, dad. Please don't do anything like that again.' She pulled away and looked into his pale blue eyes.

'I'm sorry, Pip. Apparently, I let Ginger out and then went looking for him. I say apparently because I can't remember... Pippa, there's something I need to tell you, but I don't want you to get upset because it's under control and being slowed down by medication.' Pippa bit her lower lip to stop it from trembling. 'I have dementia.'

Tears fell again for the second time within minutes. Pippa tried her best to keep her voice even, but her brimming feelings got the better of her and she had to swallow past the large lump in her throat to speak. When she did, her voice cracked with emotion. 'I'm going to be here for you, dad. I'm going nowhere.'

His face lit up. 'You're not going back to Ireland?'

She shook her head. 'Nope, I'm selling my apartment and buying a pub with my fiancée.'

Brett's brow pulled together, forming a line. 'Fiancée? Buying a pub?' He looked at Ned who shrugged with a look of bewilderment. Then he looked at Morgan who was grinning like a Cheshire cat. She turned to look at Oliver, and Brett followed her gaze.

Oliver was grinning sheepishly. 'I hope you don't mind, Brett, but I've just asked for your daughter's hand in marriage.'

Brett's face beamed. 'That's the best news I've heard in a long time.' He extended his hand to Oliver who accepted it immediately. Brett shook it and then pulled Oliver in for a hug, patting his back. 'Welcome to the family, Oliver.'

Ned joined in with the patting. 'Congratulations.'

Morgan pulled Pippa in for a hug. 'I'm so happy for you, Kiddo. I spotted your string engagement ring as soon as you walked in. I'm guessing this was a spur-of-the-moment proposal?'

Pippa grinned and nodded. 'It was just like the proposal I've had in a reoccurring dream my whole life.'

'Where's my Princess?' Pippa turned to face her father. He had his arms open wide. 'Let your old Pa give you a congratulatory kiss.' Pippa walked into his arms and he kissed her on the forehead. 'Marie is so proud of you, Pip. She's smiling down from heaven above right now.' A happy sob escaped Pippa's lips.

'My turn,' said Oliver. 'You don't know how long I've waited to hold your daughter in my arms, Brett.'

Oliver grabbed Pippa's wrist and pulled her to him. He cupped her face and kissed her again. Cheers rang out. Oliver lifted his face with a grin. 'Drinks all around.'

Brett roared with laughter. 'Cheeky beggar. Your name is not above the door yet. I'll call this...*champagne* all around.'

*

Book 2 in Love in Seagull Bay series is titled, Tammy's Tearoom in Seagull Bay.

*

To get the epilogue for Coming Home to Seagull Bay, check out the **Clean Romance** tab on her other pen name's website: **www.croc.com**

Smokey Sausage and five bean stew by Paul Watters, served at the dog competition.

440g five bean salad (can rinsed under cold water)

440g of smoked sausage (sliced)

4 large potatoes (peeled, rinsed and cut into chunks)

2 large sweet potatoes (peeled. Rinsed and cut into chunks)

2 large onions (peeled and diced)

4 carrot (peeled and diced)

4 sticks of cclery (rinsed and diced)

2 cloves of garlic (crushed)

1/2 teaspoon of smoked paprika

1 teaspoon of dried thyme

1 teaspoon of cumin

1 teaspoon of dried rosemary

2 tablespoons of tomato puree

2 beef stock cubes

4 pints of water

Fresh flat leaf parsley chopped for garnish

This is a very simple one pot wonder. It's a good family meal or something made quickly when you get home from work and can keep in the fridge after cooking for a few days.

First of all gather a large pot and add a drizzle of olive oil. Add the sliced sausage along with the onions, celery and carrot cook for a few minutes. Add the garlic and spices and cook for a few minutes. Add the potatoes and tomato puree and mix well add the beef stock and water and bring to the boil and simmer until vegetables is soft (chefs tip add a little Worcestershire sauce at the last minute for a depth of flavour and colour and season with salt and pepper). Now enjoy.

The author or Paul Watters takes no responsibility for what you feed yourself.

Follow Paul Watters for more tasty recipes on Instagram[1] or Facebook[2].

---

1. https://www.instagram.com/watterspaul/
2. https://www.facebook.com/Paulwattersfood

Don't miss out the fur babies.

Paul Watters Smokey Sausage Five bean Casserole for dogs

440g five bean salad (can rinsed under cold water)

440g of smoked sausage or high percentage meat sausage (sliced)

4 large potatoes (peeled, rinsed and cut into chunks)

2 large sweet potatoes (peeled. Rinsed and cut into chunks)

4 carrot (peeled and diced)

4 sticks of celery (rinsed and diced)

1 teaspoon of dried thyme

1 teaspoon of cumin (dogs can eat this in small amounts)

1 teaspoon of dried rosemary

2 beef stock cubes (saltless or use pure beef stock)

4 pints of water

Half the recipe's measurements for a smaller batch.

Onions, garlic, tomato puree and paprika have been taken out for the human version of the recipe, as they are deemed toxic for dogs' health.

This recipe can be made alongside your own to pamper your pooch, but make sure all the ingredients are okay for your dog before feeding it to him/her.

The author or Paul Watters takes no responsibility for what you feed your pet.

As we know, animals can't eat all of our human foods, so the recipe used in the story has been changed to accommodate the canine tummy.

*

Michelle Hill writes under another pen name. Check out C. Y. Croc, ONLY if you are *also* a reader of scifi action packed **dark** romance with wide-open door scenes.

Printed in Great Britain
by Amazon